To Any Soldier

TO ANY SOLDIER

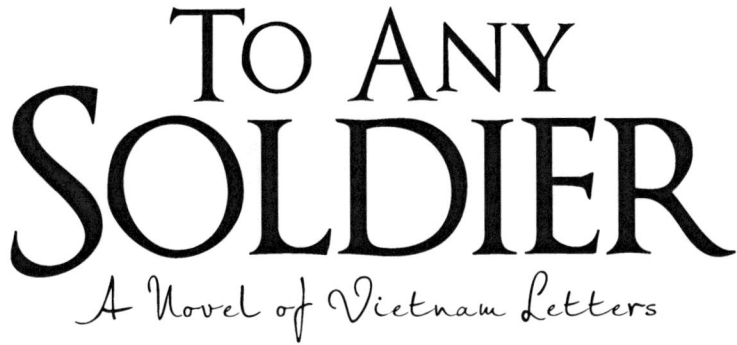

A Novel of Vietnam Letters

G. C. HENDRICKS &
KATHRYN WATSON QUIGG

TO ANY SOLDIER
A NOVEL OF VIETNAM LETTERS

Certain characters in this work are historical figures, and certain events portrayed did take place. However, this is a work of fiction. All of the other characters, names, and events as well as all places, incidents, organizations, and dialogue in this novel are either the products of the author's imagination or are used fictitiously.

iUniverse books may be ordered through booksellers or by contacting:

iUniverse
1663 Liberty Drive
Bloomington, IN 47403
www.iuniverse.com
1-800-Authors (1-800-288-4677)

Because of the dynamic nature of the Internet, any web addresses or links contained in this book may have changed since publication and may no longer be valid. The views expressed in this work are solely those of the author and do not necessarily reflect the views of the publisher, and the publisher hereby disclaims any responsibility for them.

Any people depicted in stock imagery provided by Thinkstock are models, and such images are being used for illustrative purposes only. Certain stock imagery © Thinkstock.

ISBN: 978-1-4917-6873-0 (sc)
ISBN: 978-1-4917-6874-7 (e)

Library of Congress Control Number: 2015912753

Print information available on the last page.

iUniverse rev. date: 10/30/2015

To all who serve in foreign wars and
to all who wait for them at home

Prologue

He stepped into the classroom wearing blue jeans, a white western-style dress shirt, cowboy boots, and a John Deere baseball cap. Jay Fox was still an imposing figure at fifty-six, a big man, strong and weathered from his years in the sun, his hair cut short, military-style, his face clean shaven. He moved like a soldier as he strode across the front of the room looking at the maps of Vietnam, studying the twenty-five adolescent faces, and absorbing the quiet that followed his introduction. Moving methodically, he turned to the class. "This room looks a lot like our Ready Room in Da Nang. It was about this size with maps all around the walls just like your maps. We sat about where you're sitting while the colonel told us about our mission for the night."

Jay looked out at the faces, faces not much younger than his when he flew over two hundred missions in Vietnam. A young girl with dark blonde hair shyly smiled at him, tossing her head the way *she* had, taking him back.

He quickly moved his eyes to the rest of the class. "It's four o'clock in the afternoon. We've showered after our naps and put on our flight suits. Every man is serious, dead serious, focused as we listen to the briefing. My navigator, Randy, is by my side, and my A-6 is being fueled and readied for the midnight run, checked and rechecked." Jay walked to the maps and pointed to Da Nang. "This is where I was stationed." He turned to the group and explained, "For two hours we listen, ask questions, and plan for the bombing run. We are marine attack pilots and navigators, the best the US has to offer. Ready for whatever comes our way; ready for our *last supper.*" Jay looked down and swallowed. "That's what we called it because we never knew for sure if we would be coming back," he said. "After supper we wrote letters or watched movies or slept, anything to pass the time and get us to midnight. I always wore a red bandanna around my neck, my good-luck charm from a girl back home." Jay cleared his throat and stared directly at *her*, almost through *her*.

"Every night at eleven thirty, I checked my plane, the one that said Lieutenant Jay Fox and later Captain Jay Fox on the canopy rails. I talked to the engine man, walked around the tires looking for tread wear, rubbed the nose, and then walked back to the Ready Room to suit up and get any final instructions or changes that may have come in during the last few hours. It was a ritual, almost like a prayer, each day, exactly the same." Jay took a deep breath, looked down at his watch, and began again. "At the stroke of midnight, Randy and I strapped on that sixty thousand pounds of metal, fuel, and bombs and began the reason for living, flying a bombing run in Vietnam. It was like a giant dodgeball game in the air to run through a barrage of firepower, deliver our bombs, and lift above the antiaircraft artillery, sweating and frightened by the guns that almost got us." Jay wiped his brow as if he was reliving the scene; his eyes peered up to the left. He caught himself, pulled his gaze back to the class, and said, "Our mission accomplished, our enemy destroyed, we returned to base and headed to the Officers' Club for beer and whiskey with the other returning pilots. We were comrades, saluting and celebrating another day and mourning those who wouldn't celebrate again."

Jay then smiled, breathed deeply, and said, "The cook fixed us grits, and that's what they called me and Randy, *Grit Flight.* After breakfast, we slept, sunbathed, ran for exercise, or wrote letters to the folks back home, to the girls we hoped to see on our return. We didn't have a lot of time to think about what we were doing. We worked hard every day, treated everybody with respect, and ate our last supper each night."

Later that evening, Jay called to his wife as he strode out the back door—told her he was going to the storage shed to go through some Vietnam letters. He explained that speaking to *that* class made him want to look up a few things. Jay moved slowly to the shed, his arms and legs sore from repairing the back pasture fence that afternoon. His lantern was swinging beside him while his dogs, Alpha and Harley, danced toward a new adventure. After propping the lantern on top of the file cabinet, Jay turned a wooden crate on its side so he could sit straddling the file drawer. The dogs settled at his feet. He knew which drawer to pull, and from there he went directly to some old letters tied with string. There were the family letters, the friends' letters, and then there were *her* letters, wrapped in a clean but tattered red bandanna, just where he had placed them with the copies of his own letters spaced in between. The guys had teased him about keeping copies of the letters, but that's how Captain Fox was, meticulous in every detail, knowing every word he sent out along with every detail of every mission. Jay rubbed his eyes in the soft flickering light, put on his bifocals, and opened the first letter.

January 15, 1968

PO Box 534
Sylvan Lewis College
Parkville, North Carolina

To Any Soldier,

One of the girls on my hall said lots of soldiers don't get much mail. She's always writing to her boyfriend in Vietnam, so I guess she knows. I thought I would do my duty and send a little news from the home front to cheer you. I feel awkward writing to someone I don't know, but I like to write letters, so here goes. I can't imagine what it's like to be so far from home and in such danger. I've never been homesick a day in my life, probably because I've never traveled much, and I go to a college that is only fifty-five miles from where I grew up, so I know I can go home anytime I want.

The war seems so far away from my everyday life—going to classes, studying, and taking time out to play. I have a friend from high school who is going to Vietnam in February to be a medic on a helicopter. I hope you never get to meet Andy, because you'll probably be wounded if you do. Perhaps the war will seem more real to me when he is over there.

I'm a college freshman. I turned nineteen in December. I've lived all my life in the South, but I look forward to traveling when I get out. (Sounds like I'm in prison, doesn't it?) As a matter of fact, I'm hoping to go to Maine this summer to work in a national park. Mark, the guy I'm dating, has worked at Acadia National Park for the past three years, and he thinks it would be great if I applied to be a waitress in a fancy but rustic restaurant in the park called the Jordan Pond House. It is near Rockefeller Gardens, and Mark said Nelson comes by for lunch several times each summer. I don't think our politics are the same, but it's kind of fun to meet famous people. Last fall I sat beside Gerald Ford at a football game, and he shared his 1933 All-America blanket with me. His son is in the same fraternity with the guy I was dating, and we just happened to be seated beside him. I didn't know he was house minority leader in Congress. I just knew he was someone's dad who saw me shivering and shared his blanket. My New Year's resolution is to become more politically aware.

I grew up on a farm in a little town named Larkinton, twenty-five miles north of Raleigh. It's a huge place, a real metropolitan city. There's a population sign by the road as you enter downtown that reads 1,392, and it's been the same number for as long as I can remember. I guess births and deaths equal out, or maybe it wasn't worth the cost of a new sign when the numbers changed. Most of the people work in one of the two mills in town or in one of the few small businesses. Others are small farmers like my father, who raised cows until he got sick and Mother sold the herd. Daddy was interbreeding Polled Herefords with Charolais, to produce bigger beef cattle with less fat. The baby calves were usually white like Charolais and about a third larger than the red-and-white Herefords. My brother-in-law bought a few of Daddy's cows and rented the pastures from Mother. This year one of those cows had twin calves. Daddy would have been so excited. He used to talk about wanting twin calves, but in all his years raising cattle, he never had a cow who delivered twins.

I'm the youngest of three. My two sisters are married and have two children each. They both married young, but I plan to finish college and work a while before I settle down. My mother still lives on the farm. My father died of cancer last year. I was salutatorian of my high school class of forty (big deal!), and I was chosen Best All Around and Best Looking. They didn't have a lot of choices with only forty seniors. I'm proudest of the Best All Around superlative. My high school was tiny, and a lot of people went steady, so there weren't a lot of options for casual dating. I dated one person pretty seriously the summer I was sixteen, but he went back to college, and that was that.

It's been so much fun to be in college. My first roommate last fall was a real partier. I liked her okay, but she used to party all night in our room. Often I would search for the room and bed of one of the partiers and go there so I could get some sleep. Needless to say, my grades weren't the best during my first semester. Jena, a good friend of mine, had a roommate who left school to get married after exams, so I moved into her room for the second semester. At least I can get some sleep now. Last fall I ran for class senator and won. I've also been chosen to be in the Most Popular Freshman Girl contest, and the dance is to be held this weekend. I've been dating lots of different people, but the guy who works in Maine each summer has been the most fun to be with lately. He's a senior and is majoring in English.

Another of my best friends here is a super activist named Annie. Her boyfriend goes to another school, and he's involved in one cause after another. He and a male friend entered a kissing contest to prove how ridiculous the taboos are regarding same-sex affection. I don't always agree with Annie, but she has certainly made me look at the world differently. I think I saw the world like a mule with blinders on when I was in Larkinton. I've only been gone for six months, and it feels like I don't belong there anymore. Lots of nights, we stay up way past midnight talking. At least now when I come back to my room, I can go to sleep without a party. Do you ever feel like the service has changed you?

I hope you like the picture. My hair is a little shorter now, but my face still looks the same! I'm tall for a girl, five feet seven and one half inches. How tall are you? Send me a picture. Write when you can. I look forward to getting to know you through your letters. Tell me all about you!

Best Regards,
Ashley Beth Justice

25 Jan '68

Dear Ashley Beth,

Your "Any Soldier" mail was on the bulletin board yesterday. Your handwriting reminds me of my sister's, so I brought your letter back to the hooch with me. (Hooch is what we call any living quarters. It could be a Southeast Asia hooch, a wooden building with screen walls up on stilts; or a Quonset hut, curved metal top; or a barracks, a large, wooden building on the ground with a concrete base. I'm in a Quonset.) Thanks for making the effort to send some word.

I am a marine. I drive the fast movers, the heavy haulers. I'm an attack pilot. I find the enemy. I define the enemy. I establish an area of operation. I close with and destroy the enemy regardless of weather, terrain, or proximity of enemy fire. If I am able, I return to my base. My navigator is from South Carolina. He was raised on a farm down there. We got here about the same time and started flying together, as a crew, because we don't have to talk to each other to make things do right. We work together like we were raised together. Randy has a grin that never leaves him, so you always think he's got something up his sleeve. He's the best bombardier/ navigator in the Marine Corps. He's married to his high school sweetheart, Diane, and they've got a little girl. He talks about his gals all the time.

Our tactical call sign is "Grit," and we are the only ones over here who get to eat grits for breakfast. A man who owns a store back home near Piedmont sends me a five-pound bag of Quakers every week. I get a third. Randy, my navigator, gets a third for keeping me alive (and because he understands about grits), and the enlisted cook down at the chow hall gets a third for having our hot grits ready every morning when we get back from flying the night hops up north.

In response to your letter: first, we don't do politics over here, and nobody's heard of Gerald Ford. The only famous people around here are the enemy gunners. There's a real good enemy gunner at Mu Gia. He got our wingman two weeks ago. Every time we fly against him, he curls a few rounds over our wings, and nobody's been able to get a direct hit on his position yet. He must have some sort of hydraulic withdrawal system where he can fire his eighty-five millimeter antiaircraft artillery then push a button and scoot back into his cave on the mountain before our bombs hit him. Getting a thousand-pounder into his cave is a tough run, even for the best of us, because you have to fly straight into the mountain on the run-in. Randy and I get a shot at him tonight, so by the time you get this letter, the Mu Gia Gunner will be history, made that way by Grit. Another famous person around here is the gunner at the A Shau—not really the gunner but the man who controls the whole network of guns in the valley. His people are very good. To hit almost any target in the valley, we have to fly through the fire of four different gun positions, and their fire is perfectly coordinated. Tomorrow the A Shau gets the Alpha treatment. (Alpha is a group of mad marine airplane drivers hitting the same target or group of targets continuously for hours until those targets are beaten into submission.) Right now the A Shau gunner is the most famous person over here. Everybody is paying attention to him.

Second, I was raised in Piedmont, south of where you were raised. Ask your mother about these names: my mother was a Dabbs, her mother was a Barrett, and her mother was a Bateman, her mother was a Frost. My father's mother was a Joyner, her mother was a Taylor, and her mother was a Cartwright from Virginia. I'm sure your mother has heard some of those names, and if so, she might know some of my people. We might be kin.

Finally, I saw some of those protester people like your friend the super activist and her faggot boyfriend in Georgetown while I was stationed at Quantico, and then I saw some more of them in the airport at LA on the way over here. Those are some sick people. You need to stay away from those sick people.

Thanks again for sending some word. I'll try to write again soon. Got to go run three miles before I fly.

We're off to Mu Gia,
Jay Fox

February 3, 1968

> PO Box 534
> Sylvan Lewis College
> Parkville, North Carolina

Dear Jay Fox,

It was good to hear from you. Thanks for the snapshots of you and your plane. You are certainly leading an exciting life compared to mine. I wouldn't want the danger, but I relish the adventure and the excitement. I want to do so many things in my life. I'm just not sure one lifetime is enough to do them all. Does that make any sense to you? Sometimes I'm really afraid that I won't do any of them, that I'll wake up from a dream and be an old woman who has just existed and never really lived. At least in the midst of all the danger, you are living an adventure.

Second semester is in full swing. I've had two quizzes. I'm not sure how well I did. The laugh of the day, every day, occurs when a group of us sit around at supper and compare notes on professors. It's fun to pick on their idiosyncrasies in the safety of the dining hall. One of my teachers in a required course is a lady with no knees. Honestly, this lady's legs are the same size from the waist down, and the rolls of extra flesh make her knees fade into the background. She treats all of us like we are in fourth grade, and discovering the knee factor was the only thing that made the class bearable. Another professor, when you look at him from the back, looks exactly like the top of a pencil. He wears a flat top, and his hair is the eraser. When the pencil turns around, the eraser has a face with eyes and glasses under it. He stands in front of his Old Testament class, looks at the ceiling in the back of the classroom, and lectures nonstop. I often wondered if I wanted to ask a question how I would manage it. I thought about standing on top of a desk and jumping up and down with my hand raised just to be in his line of vision. Believe it or not, I really like this teacher. On the first test in his class last semester, I got a seventy-two. I would have been devastated except that he wrote on the top of the page, "Congratulations, highest grade in the class." He does not curve his grades, so the best I got was a hook. One man, a preacher, got a B. No one made an A, and most people made Ds. Several people failed. I know it's crazy, but I actually chose him again for the New Testament class. This class was so different from Sunday school and church because he actually wanted us to challenge our beliefs. He made me look at the Old Testament as a product of the culture. He felt there were great truths in the writing but pushed the class to go beyond a literal translation. I saw things I'd never seen before. I learned a lot, even if my grade didn't show it.

I think I told you that I was in the Most Popular Freshman Girl contest. Well, console me. I lost. The dance was sponsored by a fraternity, and they block-voted for their candidate. I was nominated by the freshman and junior classes, but the dance was attended mostly by people from the sponsoring fraternity, and students could only vote if they paid to get into the dance. Sounds like sour grapes, doesn't it? Well, it is! I had a great time at the dance, even though I was disappointed at the election. Have I told you that I love to dance? I love the Carolina shag or bop or whatever you want to call it. I also love to slow dance. What a great excuse to hug in public!

By the way, what does Tet mean? I caught a news

show the other night when I was walking through the TV room—I'm usually at supper then—and I slowed down to watch. The Tet Offensive was all the newsman could talk about. Is there a place called Hamburger Hill? The pictures looked pretty gruesome. There were lots of bodies, but the newsman said they were mostly North Vietnamese. It was good to learn you are a pilot and not on the ground. Help me really understand what's going on over there. It all seems so unreal over here.

It's snowing outside, and I think I'm the only person awake on my floor. It's so quiet and so beautiful. The streetlight shines on the snow outside my window, and the whole world is transformed. I feel like I'm in a fairyland. I wish I could run outside and play in the clear, fresh coldness. I guess if I lived in the north it wouldn't be so exciting, but this may be the only snow we get this year, and I want to savor every moment. When I was a child, I used to stand outside with my mouth open and catch the snowflakes on my tongue. My mother would make snow cream, and I would try to save some in the freezer. Invariably, it would turn to ice by summer and never live up to my hopes. I still put it in the freezer, though. I wish I could zap you some as they do on <u>Star Trek</u>. I'm sure on some of those hot, sweltering days in the jungle you could use a little bit of home. I'm not sure I'll sleep at all tonight. Every time it snows, I feel like a little kid who is getting a peek at Christmas early. All I want to do is sit by this window, look at the blizzard, pull my blanket more closely around my shoulders, and dream all those dreams I have.

I'm trying out for a play next week. Annie, my activist friend, is quite involved in the theater. She's encouraging me to take the plunge. I'm a bit nervous, but I have always wanted to do this. In high school I was in the junior class play. It was a dippy play because the teachers wouldn't let us pick anything with a message or anything risqué. Here, the plays are loaded with symbolism and sometimes quite risqué. I went to one the other night and got so caught up in the characters. When I walked outside, it was dark, and I felt disoriented. These plays make me feel free. I like this new freedom.

Speaking of my activist friend, I told her what you said, and she went into a tirade about people not knowing why they were in Vietnam and how she felt sorry for you and all those like you. She said to tell you she hopes you never need someone like her boyfriend to stand up for you, and you are homophobic, which is a sure sign that you just might be gay. You two remind me of each other. You both have prejudged the other without ever knowing that a real person is behind the facade. When you drop your next bombs, name the enemy gunner Annie, and I'm sure you'll have a direct hit. I'm really sorry people in the airports and in Georgetown have treated you without the respect you deserve. They are wrong. Annie is wrong when she fails to see you as someone who is doing his job in a tough situation, and you are wrong for writing her off without ever knowing her. I like you both.

I haven't had a chance to ask Mother about the names you mentioned. My mother's people came to America in the mid-eighteen hundreds, probably during the potato famine in Ireland. They were Scots-Irish and poor. Two brothers came, and one settled down east near Elizabeth City. The other settled somewhere else, and no one ever heard from him again. Her maiden name was Stephenson. Her mother's maiden name

14

was Worrell, and my grandfather's mother was a Griffin. That's as far back as I know. My father's people were Edwards and Browns. Your list of names sounds like your folks came over on the Southern Mayflower.

Believe it or not, I have been through Piedmont. It appears to be very much like Larkinton from what I can remember. Probably a little larger. I think my mother taught school near Piedmont in the early thirties. I can't remember the name of the place, but I'll ask her when I talk to her about the names.

You sure know how to make a girl feel good. You read my letter because my handwriting reminded you of your sister's. That's what every girl wants, to be like someone's sister. Well, I guess that makes you a pretty safe pen pal.

Since I've decided to stay awake most of the night and enjoy the snow, I had better use the time to write some other letters that I've been putting off. Tell me more about you in your next correspondence. I know you like grits, but what else do you like? I'll try to get up a care package if you'll let me know what you are missing the most from home. I'm sure my mother would make you some teacakes if I ask her. That's her specialty.

Write soon and keep safe!
Ashley Beth

18 Feb '68

Dear Ashley Beth,

We're in the monsoon. It's been raining for days. Water stands outside my hooch. The clouds are so low there is fog most of the time. This is when we earn our pay. The fighter jocks and the daytime attack jocks are standing down (not flying), staying drunk, watching movies because of the weather. But the A-6 was designed to fly in bad weather at night, down low in the mountains. We take off each morning about one. The rain never stops. We go into the clouds as soon as we lift off and fly to our targets, flying for two hours in the clouds. When you return to base and shoot an approach, you always wonder if you'll be near the runway when you break out at the bottom. But you always come out of the clouds over the approach end of the runway, and there's that one second where you have to transition from the gauges, where you've been for two hours, to the runway that looks like the midway at the state fair, all lit up. Randy is the best navigator around, so I just follow his info on my little TV screen, and we make flying in the goo look easy.

In response to your letter, during my freshman year in high school I was in a one-act play. We took the show on the road to the university, to a one-act play competition. It was a heady time; we were some hot stuff going to the university to put on our play. The story was about Eastern Europe during the war. I was a soldier. I stayed on the stage during the entire production, but I had only one line:

"Halt! Who goes there?"

"It is I, Matisse Rotha!" was the reply.

A shadowy figure with a shawl over her head emerged from the darkness. I remember that I allowed her to pass, but I don't remember much more except that we had fun, and I think about Matisse Rotha every time I see a sentry at a checkpoint around here. Someday one of the sentries is going to say to me, "Halt! Who goes there?" I can't wait to tell him about Matisse Rotha.

You think your professors are weird? We've got Major Weber. The club opens every day at 1600 hours, and everybody who's not flying goes there and drinks whiskey and prepares to dine and go to the movies. Major Weber is a big man with a dark complexion and a neat mustache, sort of a dapper fellow, and he's always there because he is a groupie and doesn't fly. After he's had two martinis, you can walk up to him and ask him what time it is, and he will rotate his left wrist and look at his watch and pour his drink on the front of his shirt. I've seen him throw three drinks on himself in one afternoon. He'll take a sip, and somebody will go up to him and say, "What time is it, Major Weber?" And Major Weber will throw the drink right on his own chest and shout out the time. Somebody asked him one day if he knows people are going to ask him for the time, why does he always keep his drink in the hand on the same side of his body where his watch is? "Procedures, Lieutenant. Procedures!"

Tet is a Gook holiday. This year we had to earn what we got. We flew twice a day for two weeks. The Gooks lost three of their main divisions and their entire support network. My squadron lost only two airplanes and one aircrew. We spoiled their little holiday, but what you are hearing and seeing in the news back home is what the leftist news pukes have decided to report back to America. They tell it the way they want it to be instead of the way it is. I keep waiting to hear about the one person in the news media who is anywhere near as professional as any of us. We put the bombs on the targets day and night. They are missing their mark.

What do I like besides grits? Every Saturday we send a cargo plane to Perth, Australia, to pick up our Sunday brunch: live lobster fresh from the reef and choice, aged Australian beef. We cook our own meat on a grill outside the Officers' Club, and we drink beer. I like Sunday brunch. Also, Randy and I like to play the guitars. We try to play at least every other day. We sing hymns, old Jimmy Rogers' songs, some hillbilly stuff both of us have known all our lives, and a few of Johnny Cash's real early songs like "Blackland Farmer" and "Going to Memphis," and Randy misses Diane, so he sings love songs about her.

Every day, rain or shine, at some time when I'm not flying, I go running for an hour. It's always hot, and no matter where I run, trucks or airplanes are buzzing past, so the conditions are not ideal, but the exercise dissipates the energy and keeps me taut, in perfect shape for flying, and I just like to run.

Don't get the impression I'm safe to write to. I am, after all, a marine airplane driver. And I have seen your picture, which brings us to the question of what I miss the most. Round-eyed women are what I miss most. I saw some when I went to sea survival training in Okinawa, but that was three months ago. While I was there, I made a transfer call to my sister and said, "Just talk," just so I could hear a girl voice.

Next to round-eyed women, I miss hamburgers the most. They try to make them at the chow hall, but it's just not the same. I have this fantasy of finishing my job here and flying my own jet across the Pacific. When I get to California, instead of landing at El Toro, I'll hang a left and fly to LA. I'll land on Hollywood Boulevard. The cars will all get out of the way. I'll fold my wings and taxi down the boulevard until I come to a hamburger joint with a drive-in window. There I will pull in and order: cheeseburger, mustard, lettuce, tomato, chili, and onions. Then I will take off and go find a round-eyed woman. Maybe I'll come to see you. I graduated in '63, so I'm nearly the same age as those boys who are seniors at your college. And why didn't they pick you as the most popular freshman girl? You come over here, and I guarantee you'll win any contest you want.

I do appreciate your letters. My folks write twice each week, and I get a few letters from old friends, but I ended all my relationships back in the world. Just a week before I left home, I lost Company C. He was named for the old McGuire Sisters' song "Boogie Woogie Bugle Boy of Company B." When he was a puppy, he made a sound like a bugle, so we named him after the song, but we got the name wrong. He was thirteen, and he couldn't get up, see, or hear well, but he could walk. On his last day, I took off for my walk, and he struggled to his feet. From the first hill I could look back and watch him gain his balance and take those first few, stiff steps, then begin his slow, methodical walk. I could see him as he used to be, dancing ahead, running back to lick my hand, chasing a ghost rabbit or a chattering squirrel out of our pathway, always smiling (if dogs can smile), and tongue hanging out of his mouth while his dark round eyes begged for that pat on the head that would always connect us. I went ahead slowly that day, waiting for him and our connecting touch, and down the path he came. He walked a long mile with me on his last day. He was the bravest man I've ever known. So when I left home, I had broken all the ties outside my family. I wanted to be able to concentrate on my work here and not have to worry about anything back home. But it's nice to hear from somebody back there who's about my age.

Semper Fi,
Jay

March 3, 1968

PO Box 534
Sylvan Lewis College
Parkville, North Carolina

Dear Jay,

It was so good to get your letter! It has been over a month, and I was afraid something had happened on one of your missions. My anxiety intensified a week ago when I walked down my hall and saw the girl who had given me the Any Soldier address slumped against the door of her room. Her name is Janie, and I know her but not real well. She is a big girl, not very attractive, and a bit rough. She never dates on campus and goes home most weekends. I stopped to ask if she was okay. She stared past me and didn't answer. One of her friends came up and steered me down the hall. She said Janie's boyfriend was missing in action. I felt really helpless, and that's when I began to worry about you. I should have known the Redneck Baron would be okay. That's what Annie calls you! I'm sending you a red bandanna to bring you luck. It's been ceremonially blessed by all my friends. I think I'll call you Red Baron and leave off the "neck" part.

So you're only four years older than me. I thought you might be five or six years older. After all, you're a lieutenant, and you fly planes and fraternize with majors. I'm impressed! I don't even drink. I have tasted beer at several parties but decided if I had to cultivate a taste for that stuff, well, I just decided to sip my Cokes and keep a natural high. So far I've managed to stay out of trouble that way.

I loved your hamburger fantasy. Why don't you

just grind up some of that aged Australian beef and make your own hamburger. It's worth a shot.

When you fly over to LA, and then you fly to see me, I want you to park the plane right in front of the dorm. Come and call for me at the desk. Wear your leather flight jacket with a scarf at your neck, just like in the old movies. Speak with a foreign accent and be very aloof. I'll come down dressed in jodhpurs, knee-high boots, a white blouse, and leather jacket. We'll spend the entire evening flying. I've only flown once in my entire life, and never in the cockpit. Maybe you'll even give me a flying lesson and let me take the controls. I'm a quick study!

We'll land in front of the dorm at 11:55 p.m., just before the dorm is locked, when all the couples are kissing good night and trying to see who is dating whom. You'll jump out of the plane, lift me down, and walk me to the door, while everybody is looking, of course. You'll trace my lips with your finger, put your scarf around my neck, pull me toward you, and kiss me hard. Then you'll stride back to the plane. Several girls who think they're hot stuff will say, "Who is he?" And I'll say, doe-eyed, "His name is Matisse Rotha," and then I'll move quickly up the stairs. What do you think? Will it play? I'm going out tomorrow to the Army Surplus store to get my flight jacket. Call me from the hamburger joint in LA.

Mother begs me to come home every weekend. I know she's lonely since Daddy died, but I just can't go every weekend, or I'd miss everything here. Sometimes I feel so guilty when she calls.

Your story about Company C reminded me of my cat Laramie. He was an orange tabby who had lost an eye after being hit by a car when he was one.

21

His head was misshapen, and he could, of course, only see out of one eye, but he was the first cat I ever belonged to. I used to hang him on the screen door by his front claws and tell him to love me. He would lean over and butt into me. We used to sit on one end of the carport, and whenever Daddy's hounds would come near the porch, I would say, "Sic 'em, Laramie." He would wait at the edge of the porch. When a dog came too near, Laramie would pounce on the dog's back and ride like a rodeo star as the dog yelped and fled from the carport. Most days after school, I would go for long walks in the pasture. My dog and Laramie would always be with me. Laramie would scream for the first fifty yards until I stopped so he could dig in the dirt and attend to his needs. Then he would scoot up ahead of me, racing with the dog, each day seeking another exciting adventure. I'll never forget the day he died. He must have had a stroke or heart attack. He managed to crawl up onto the front steps, as close to my room as he could get. We found him stretched out on the stoop, clinging to life. I was thirteen and had never dealt with death. I didn't pick him up or hold him. I just left him there dying, out there on the front stoop. If I could go back to that day, I would cradle him in my arms until he breathed his last breath. He taught me so much about unconditional love, and I'll always regret not holding him one last time.

Last weekend I decided to go home, and I rode with this guy who lives about thirty-five miles north of Larkinton. He works at a radio station in his hometown on weekends. He's a sophomore, and I know him because he's the lab assistant for my Zoology class. Milton's been offering me rides home ever since he learned I was from Larkinton. He wears his pants up under his armpits, carries a slide rule, and wears horn-rimmed glasses. Another guy who looks a lot like Milton, except he has curly hair, always rides with him. They are both short and speak in clipped, measured phrases. I sat in the backseat, and they sat in the front. I pretended to read, sleep, and study so I wouldn't have to converse more than necessary. Every time we would cross a railroad track, the guy on the passenger side would beat on the dash while the driver swerved the car. Then they would look back at me and laugh maniacally at my reaction. This didn't just happen on the trip home but also on the trip back to campus. Do you know there are three railroad tracks between Larkinton and Parkville? My roommate, Jena, has found me laughing hysterically several times since last weekend, whenever I heard a train whistle. She's contemplating having me committed if I accept another ride from this clown.

Mother said she knew some Cartwrights when she taught in Franklin, Virginia. There are also some Barrettes who live out in the country from Larkinton, but she didn't know any of the other names.

I must confess I had a problem with one part of your last letter. When you talked about the enemy as nonhuman, Gooks, it really made me sad. I know these people are our enemy, and they will kill you if you don't kill them, but they are human beings. Please don't get angry with me like you did Annie. I'm not like her, and I'm not judging you, but I am having a hard time with that phrase. I have a hard time when I see a dead animal on the highway. I even hate to kill bugs. To think of killing people, well, you have to do what you have to do. I'm just sorry you and the enemy have to be in that situation. I hope this conflict can soon be resolved so you and all the others can come home. It makes me question God and where he is in all this. How can people believe he is on our side and pray to him for our boys' safety? Are we the chosen people just like the people of Israel? Are you David stoning the giant Goliath, or are we the giants stoning the little guy? How does God pick sides? Why does one pilot live and another die? I hope you don't mind my honesty. I admire your courage and your expertise. I just don't understand.

Have you been to college? How did you get to be a commissioned officer? You must be an exceptional pilot to be a lieutenant at twenty-three. I want so much to do something exciting with my life. The closest I've come to excitement is the play I'm rehearsing. I love working on this play. Next week we give three performances. I play a social worker who goes to see a family. When she is asked to take off her things, she immediately takes off her dress and sits around in her slip for the rest of the night. I went out and bought a black slip so I'd feel less naked on stage. My mother had a cow when I told her, but she resigned herself to the artistic value of the piece (or her inability to change anything). It's an Albee play if that means anything. He wrote <u>Who's Afraid of Virginia Woolf</u>. It's biting satire and great fun. When you fly into LA, look me up. I'll probably be working at MGM.

Have the rains ended? It's beginning to be warm here. Spring break is only a month away, and everyone is eager to have some time off. My roommate's father has a place at a North Carolina beach. Several of us are going there for a few days. He also has a boat, and I plan to learn to slalom, if the water isn't too cold. I do pretty well on two skis, can kick one ski off, but I haven't been able to get up on one yet.

Thanks for your last letter. I felt like there was a real person behind that letter. I'm glad you're not safe to write to.

Take care, Red Baron,
Ashley

PS: What in the world is Semper Fi?

March 12, 1968

Dear Jay,

I just couldn't wait for your letter to tell you. I got accepted to work as a waitress at the Jordan Pond House in Acadia National Park near Bar Harbor, Maine! Can you believe it? I'm going to work with college students from all over the country and actually live a thousand miles from home all summer. Mark tells me the park is on Mt. Desert Island. He says many of the customers live in huge summer homes around the shore. The rich summer people don't tip too well, but the tourists don't mind tipping. Girls who worked there last summer made over a thousand dollars in just nine weeks of waitressing. That would really help with school next year. Some people have gotten great tips serving a meal to one customer. I am supposed to be there by June 15. School ends here on May the twenty-first. I can hardly believe it's just three months away. When I think about tea and popovers, I start speaking in a British accent.

My friends are a little jealous that I'm getting to do something so fun this summer. Annie is going to work in an ink pen factory in her hometown. Jena hasn't gotten a job yet. My mother was both happy and sad for me. Of course she wanted me to come home, but she gave me her permission to apply for this job. I just felt like I had to get away this year, or she would be more dependent on me than she already is. If Daddy were alive, I'm sure he wouldn't let me go. He was always so afraid something would happen to us. Mother's philosophy is that one is only young once. She doesn't want me to regret not having done things when I get older. She wishes she had continued to teach after she got married, but Daddy wanted her to stay home, so she followed his wishes. Now she feels she missed out on something. But I get to go to Maine. I wrote her a long letter and thanked her for understanding.

Mark works as the kitchen supervisor and has gone back every year for three years. He says it's pretty cold up there in the summer. It will be strange to wear sweaters and jeans all summer. We have to wear these cute little pink or yellow waitress costumes while we are at work. He says the staff celebrates mock Christmas and New Year's. Each person has one day off every week, and four or five people usually wind up with the same day. I hope somebody with a car has the same day off I have. I'm so excited I can hardly stand it. When you make your flight to LA, you'll have to fly north to Maine instead of across to North Carolina. I'll make sure you have a place to stay, maybe on one of the yachts in Northeast Harbor.

By the way, when is your tour over? Will you be stationed at Camp Lejeune when you return? That's only a few hours from Parkville. Perhaps next fall you could come up some weekend to a dance or some other campus activity. You and Annie could spar with each other, and I could bandage the wounded.

Ain't it great? This little old country girl is finally getting out of the country!

Be safe, Red Baron,
Ashley Beth

17 March '68

AB

So ... summer in Maine, huh? Sounds good. Any place with cool air sounds good. And it's a good work situation. The work has the potential to offer up some camaraderie. That's what the Marine Corps is all about—the group effort and the satisfaction of being a part of the group. Everybody going in the same direction, working for the same goal, an important goal.

They always have to keep somebody qualified to drop nukes, just in case we need to drop some on somebody, so they picked me to go to the school in Japan where they teach nuke-dropping tactics to American airplane drivers. I flew up there on a cargo plane, in the back with the cargo and thirty other officers and some enlisted men on their way to schools. We flew at low altitude over the ocean. About an hour after takeoff, we hit severe turbulence. It was hot back there with the cargo, and the airplane was groaning and jerking, never stopping, bouncing in all directions, and finally this enlisted navy boy erupted in projectile vomiting. It took less than a minute for most of the passengers to start throwing up. Big mess. I held my cookies, but it was not a fun flight.

There were four of us in the nuke class: two air force pilots, a navy pilot, and me. The faculty was top-heavy; several colonels and majors were there to teach us new guys how to fly the drop. They had everything planned out for the whole week except for Wednesday afternoon, which was scheduled for free time. By Wednesday at noon, I was ready for some free time, so I cleaned up and put on my civvies and got some cash and headed for town. The town was Hiroshima. I took the fast train about twenty miles north. The train was full of people but moved on time, very efficient. I got off in town near ground zero where the old guys had dropped the nuke. There was a monument, and at the monument there was a book where travelers from all over the world could record their thoughts. There were entries like "Want that this cannot happen again" and "Never was suffering so great." Then there was the entry from some American serviceman, "Tough shit." Afterward, I decided to catch a movie. The closest theater was a double feature, with dubbed-in Japanese voices and English subtitles. If you take the trip as a whole, it was an interesting time.

Thanks for the red bandanna. The enclosed picture shows how I've incorporated it into my wardrobe. Goes nice with the survival vest, don't you think? It does actually serve a purpose tied around my neck. In spite of the climate controls in the cockpit, it gets hot during a combat hop. A lot is going on in the cockpit, and Randy and I don't have time to worry about being too hot. Sweat saturates the bandanna, and the wet rag cools my neck and throat. So I wear it on every hop now. Please don't miss the symbolic significance of carrying your colors into battle.

They say we will be leaving in the fall. Here's my new itinerary. Land in LA and get the burger, then taxi with wings folded to Vegas for a few days of cheap food, free shows, and maybe a little booze. I could find a local airport and sell rides in a combat jet to raise some cash. Then I want to take off with a full load of fuel and fly the Grand Canyon. I flew her before I came over here. I was on a cross-country hop, a low-level training mission across Arizona. I was near the canyon, and I had never flown her, so I flew her at four hundred knots, a thousand feet below the north rim east to west. In the midst of it all, I promised myself I would fly her again after the war. So I've got to do that. Then I'll probably drive the airplane, wings folded, to Parkville, just for fun, and you and I will take in a drive-in movie, maybe another burger.

You asked me about the killing. Since you are not here, that's probably a normal question. But if you were here, or at any war, you would understand that killing is a part of war. People have always had wars because it's an effective way to work out our differences. There's usually an obvious winner in the end, and it's over, no lingering questions. War seems to have become an integral part of who we are. If we end war, do we also give up compassion and the ability to love? Life is an equation, you know. Remove war and killing, and what other factors change? I don't dislike the Gooks. I have huge respect for them, and they respect me. War is something people do. Since I'm an airplane driver, I am removed from the carnage. I destroy my target and come back to my hooch for a hot beer and a few minutes in the hot morning sun before I snuggle into my air-conditioned room for my morning sleep.

I am in the hot morning sun phase right now, sitting in a folding chair in the sand on top of my bunker. It's right next to my hooch, and it's where I'm supposed to run to in the middle of the night when the Gooks start lobbing rockets into Da Nang. I usually just roll out of my rack in the hooch and lie on the floor. A direct hit by a rocket will get you no matter where you are, and anything that hits nearby will just stun you from the shock of the blast, unless a flying object gets you. So why get up and run outside to get to the bunker? But the bunker is where the rules say we're supposed to be. The bunker is a bunch of fifty-five-gallon metal barrels filled with sand and arranged in a square. Then metal roofing is laid across the barrels. Then the sand is dug out of the square and put on the roof. The result is a square, partially submerged room surrounded by, protected by sand, into which a person can go to survive a rocket attack. Or in my case, a bunker is a big pile of dirt that I can sit on in my folding chair and work on my tan. What we're after here is the perfect tan. I wear only a jock strap so I have few lines, and my tan is gorgeous. You can't see the tan in the picture because of the flight gear, but this is definitely the best tan I've ever had.

You asked me how I got to be a pilot. I got sent to college without a reason to go there. When I got to college, I looked around, and I didn't see anything I was interested in, and I didn't see anybody around me, faculty, staff, or student, who would ever really do anything, and then I saw the Blue Angels. It was on a Saturday, a beautiful day in the fall. I thought it might be interesting to go to the air show, and I parked about a mile from the airport and followed the crowd. The crowd was huge and was roped off on the edge of a taxiway. Some army people jumped out of airplanes, and some old airplanes flew by. Then the Blue Angels put on their show. That's what I wanted to do. I wanted to do what they were doing. What they were doing was difficult and important. So I quit college and joined the Marine Corps and got me a jet.

By the way, semper fi is an abbreviation for semper fidelis, from the Latin, loosely translated meaning always faithful.

I have my quota of tan for the day. I need to sleep. Last night was very scary, lots of lights in the sky, and tonight I return to the same gun positions. We evidently did not destroy them all last night, and we need to destroy them all.

Semper Fi,
J

March 24, 1968

Dear J,

Your letters confuse me. I love the pretending and the playing, but I can't figure you out. You read the statements in the Hiroshima book at the monument, and you take them lightly. You talk about war as if it is some game. You pound the draft dodgers for having a different belief from you. You talk about respect, and then you call people who are different from you a derogatory name, and it's really a stretch for me to think that war is an effective way to work out differences. Get real! Do you really expect me to believe that getting rid of war would also end compassion and love? I know the whole situation must be awful, and you may have to respond this way to deal with the job you have, but it seems for someone your age, you are pretty set in your ways with no room for other opinions. I guess that's my greatest flaw. I try too hard to understand where the other fellow is coming from before I make a decision. I probably wouldn't last two weeks over there, but I'm not sure I could live with myself if I didn't try to understand. Blast me if you want for being naïve, but I have thought a lot about Vietnam and what is happening there. I am not like the protesters who spit at returning soldiers. I admire you for your bravery and for doing what you are commanded to do, but I am not sure we should be over there. I keep thinking about the verse in Matthew, "Blessed are the peacemakers, for they shall be called the sons of God."

Thanks for the throw-up story. I am eager to hear from you, but you can spare me a few details!

I sat down in English class today, and my good buddy, Ricky, who is planning to become a lawyer, started commenting about Johnson's decision not to run. We both were completely surprised by his televised announcement the night before. Neither of us ever expected him to drop out of the race for president. It should be an interesting race without an incumbent running. Ricky and I both wondered who will get the nomination.

Tell me about your family. What does your father do? Are your parents together? Do you believe in God? I'm sure it must be hard when you see so much carnage to believe in anything. Again, I don't know what I would do in your situation. All I can think of is the quote about "There are no atheists in foxholes." Perhaps you have to be your own god in the cockpit. Anyone with the perfect tan must be a god, at least in his own mind!

I think I am going to transfer to a larger college. I like the idea of being incognito. (Something a small town like Larkinton and a small college like Sylvan Lewis don't offer.) I had planned to go to a larger college before Daddy got sick with cancer, but I felt like I had to go closer by, not knowing what was going to happen. When I got accepted by the university, I had already sent fifty dollars to Sylvan Lewis, so what it really came down to was a little bit of money and a dying father. I'll probably stay here through my sophomore year; take the required courses for university and then transfer. How did you free yourself to think differently from the small-town way people think in Piedmont?

Thanks for wearing my colors into battle. This is not a very up letter to send to a marine who is just doing his duty. I promise my next letter won't be such a downer.

Keep safe,
Ashley Beth

29 March '68

Dear Ashley Beth,

My daddy is a preacher, and my mother is a preacher's wife. We're Southern Baptists. I'm the baby. I have two older sisters who are married and working, and the parents are pastoring at a little country church. I feel real comfortable with all the God stuff, having been around the church all my life. I would hang around the church offices while Daddy worked on his sermons. He was an Old Testament preacher, and since the church was big and built of brick and there were massive steps and walkways and big brick buttresses holding back dirt, it was like a place in the Old Testament stories—you know, those cities that were destroyed by trumpets. While Daddy wrote sermons, I played Bible. It was always more of an oral history to me than a spiritual awakening. I was always more attracted to the stories than I was to the lessons. So when you say "it must be hard when you see so much carnage to believe in anything," you must remember, since I am where I am, doing what I am doing, I am part of the story. The symbolism and the meaning and the lessons of all this gets lost here in the chaos of the diesel smoke and jet-fuel fumes and the concussion waves from the rocket blasts at night. And if I remember correctly the stories my daddy told in church, there were some hard-core kick-ass dudes in the Old Testament. And in the midst of carnage, those old boys believed in their faith, and their faith was in their inspiration and their strength. So, sure, I believe in God, the inspiration for all this, and I believe in my own abilities, my strength.

As for the peacemakers being the sons of God, somebody else said the meek shall inherit the earth, and somebody else said the world belongs to the believers. Peacemakers, meek, believers, who are you going to listen to. All that New Testament stuff is kinda confusing to me.

You also asked how I freed myself to think differently from the small town of Piedmont. I already thought differently. For a long time, I thought there was something wrong with me. Then after I started flying, I realized I just had to get away from Piedmont so I could blossom. They always talk about southern ladies blossoming; well, southern boys have to blossom too. And if you think differently from the people around you, the best place to blossom is somewhere else. I've blossomed here at the war.

People behave differently in a time of war, and people show more of themselves, because war is more dramatic than simple, everyday existence. War makes reality more prominent. My life here is very serious. So it is nice to be able to be not-so-serious in my letters to you, and I thank you for that. Please don't let me scare you away. And don't feel shackled. Make a logical plan and follow the plan. You can do that.

Semper Fi,
Jay

April 5, 1968

Dear Blossoming Son of a Preacher Man,

You sure don't sound like a PK. I, too, am a Southern Baptist. Mama and Daddy are too. They didn't attend church much, so the man down the road used to take my sisters and me when I was small. Daddy used to tell a story about a preacher at my home church way before I came into the world. I think this incident was a defining moment for Daddy and made him lose faith in the church. A preacher once visited him asking for money for the building fund. Daddy gave him a donation, and when he saw the amount on the check, the preacher came back. He said, "Mr. Justice, this is not enough. I had you down for a much larger donation." That was the last donation he ever got from Daddy.

I think Daddy's religion was fox hunting. He always kept a pack of hounds in a pen not far from the house. Many nights I can remember being lulled to sleep by the group howl. He and several men would go out late at night and follow the hounds in trucks. He knew the dogs so well he could pick out the leader by his bark. He could also determine a red fox from a gray just by the track while riding down a country road at forty miles an hour in his Dodge truck. Most of the dogs were friendly, but occasionally he would have one that was a bit frightening. He had this big old yellow July hound whose name was Luck. That dog was bad news from day one. He was certainly the leader of the pack and was not very fond of anyone other than Daddy. Until I was almost twelve, we had to walk about a mile after we got off the school bus to get back down to the big old white farmhouse where we lived. I was in first grade, my oldest sister was in high school, and my middle sister was in fifth grade. We all rode the bus together because our school was a union school. For some reason, the hounds were out of the pen that afternoon. As we came up over the crest of the hill and in sight of the house, Luck saw us intruding on his territory. He gathered his cohorts in crime, five to ten of the meanest hounds I've ever seen. They began to charge toward us, circling and barking and beginning to close in for the kill. My big sister grabbed my hand, told my other sister to run, and we flew like the wind down the path. We were no match for Luck and his cronies. If Mother hadn't heard the ruckus and come out with a broom, I might not be writing this letter. (Those dogs actually killed a baby mule in the back pasture one day.) Luck finally met his maker when he crawled into a man's car during a thunderstorm. He was petrified of storms. I guess he had been out on a hunt and hadn't made it home when the storm started. The man went to get in his car not knowing Luck now owned it! It didn't take the man long to find his rifle. Daddy was perturbed that the man didn't call him before the fatal shot, but we were secretly glad Luck's luck had run out.

Farming is a pretty hard life. My folks own a five-hundred-acre farm and several rental houses, but everything they made while I was growing up went right back into the farm and equipment. People in Larkinton think we have money, but I can assure you I never saw much of it. Daddy used to give Mama one hundred dollars in the fall to buy all three children school clothes, and he would say, "Get something for you too, Martha." You can imagine she had nothing left over. I remember in fourth grade she made me a blouse from a feed sack. It had these beautiful strawberries on it, and I loved that blouse. She made me a green skirt to match. I never knew I should be ashamed to wear a feed sack. Mama didn't like to sew, so I was just proud to have something she made. She used to say, "I sew in self-defense." Whatever that meant!

She can really crochet. Last year she made me this great crocheted skirt and lined it. Nobody has one like it. She even made a vest and tam to match. Jena and Annie love the outfit and wish their mothers could crochet. I've graduated from feed sacks to "Martha Justice Originals." She even makes the skirts short like I like to wear them. I never have cared particularly what people think, and I kind of like having something no one else has. When I wear my crocheted outfit, I get admiring glances from both sexes. I have this white silk blouse that clings just so, and I wear it with my crocheted skirt. There ain't no flies on me when I walk across campus in that outfit. I'll send you a picture.

There are so many things I want to do. I want to paint and draw and write, none of which I'm told lead to a livable income without someone to provide a supplement. I'm so afraid I'll spend my life doing what I have to in order to live and not what I want to do. The main occupations open to women are teaching and nursing. Neither appeals to me. If I had gone to the same air show with the Blue Angels and made the decision you made, do you think I'd be a fighter pilot in Vietnam? My daddy wouldn't even let me drive at night by myself. Sometimes I feel like an exotic bird confined to a cage only glimpsing the outside, occasionally being taken out to have my wings clipped before being placed back in the cage again. At least I'll be flying to Maine in June. I can hardly wait!

Sorry my last letter was so blue. I had just gotten back from a date with this creep; you know the kind with Russian hands and Roman fingers. I don't know why I ever went out with him, except he is very handsome, and dating him is real status on the third floor of Lassiter dorm. Now I know what Mama meant when she said, "Looks aren't everything." I want to be close to someone, but only when it feels right. You probably think I'm a baby. Can it really be special with the right person, or is that just a romantic pipe dream? You're a "blossoming" man of the world. What do I need to know that will help me?

For some reason, I feel close to you. Thank you for that. Some days I just need someone to listen. Writing to you is my way of putting some of my thoughts out there. It just feels good. Thanks for listening and for carrying my colors! You made me feel special.

Be safe,
AB

PS: This morning is so different from yesterday. Did you hear? Martin Luther King was shot while he stood on a balcony in Memphis. Some hick redneck has been arrested. Riots are everywhere. Even here in Parkville. We have a curfew tonight. Troops are on the streets. Stores downtown looted, fires started. I looked out my dorm room and saw the National Guard marching. My heart raced when I saw a young black man being detained and then roughly escorted to a big truck. This is America, the heartland, the South. It shouldn't be happening here. I've never felt afraid before, but I must say I felt scared watching the man being put in the truck. What a difference a day makes.

11 April '68

Dear Alpha Bravo,

The MLK death and the destruction that followed were real news here. Most news from back there doesn't impact here, but with the camaraderie so tight in the squadron, and about one in five of us are black, we had to notice. Yesterday I asked my engine man, Corporal Barr, the one who keeps me alive by making sure my engines are perfect, what the death and destruction was all about back home. He's from Indianapolis, and he said, "Maybe everywhere is getting like here, this place is so whacky it's spreading all over the world." I had never really thought of him as being black until we talked yesterday. I had always thought of him as the best engine man in the squadron, and we always talked in detail about the engines during my maintenance debrief after every hop. Yesterday he looked at me and said, "Those people back there don't know what they want." It mostly seems far away, like my average day seems far away to you.

Thank you for the nice letter. I knew there was, in those first few letters, a substantial person writing under the restraints of a proper southern lady. I was posturing, too, of course, being from the South myself. While the war stories I've written about are real, they didn't need to be told early on except for their shock value and to create an image of some hard warrior dude. I'm actually just a quiet boy who likes to fly jets.

You mentioned you feel close to me. It's probably because I'm so far away. You are about five hours' flying time away from California. From California to Hawaii is five and a half hours, Hawaii to Okinawa is nine and a half hours, Okinawa to Da Nang is four hours. Our clock is twelve hours ahead of yours. It is also just different here. It's hot, between 110 and 130 degrees in the daytime and 70 to 100 percent humidity. And I live on five dollars per week. It all goes for beer and tobacco. They give us a bunch of money for doing this, and mine goes to pay for a piece of land in Arizona. I saw it last summer and just had to have it—ten acres near Strawberry, where Zane Grey used to live. By the time I get through here, the land will be paid for. After I fly my A-6 through the Grand Canyon and before I land on the interstate and fold up my wings and head for Maine, I will fly over my new land. It will appear gracefully on the horizon, and I will throttle back to, say, four hundred knots, and I will ease the nose over so I am flying just above the treetops, and my new land will flash beneath me, and I will cob the power and go vertical, and at fifteen thousand feet I will go inverted and look up, and there will be my new land in the middle of the forest. Then I'll put my airplane down on the interstate and fold my wings and head for Maine. Then, of course, you probably won't feel close to me because I'll be there.

I loved your story about the homemade clothes. When I was little, my daddy was the preacher. We lived in a tobacco farming community where nobody had a whole lot. Mama made all our clothes until one Sunday morning before church a group of uppity ladies went to Daddy's study while he was working on his sermon and told him they weren't going to have their preacher's children going to public school wearing tow sacks! Right before I came over here, Daddy was telling that story again, and I asked him what he told those ladies. He said he didn't remember, but he did preach that morning on the evils of rushing in, of going into a situation without the proper meditation. And the following morning, everybody was out shopping for children's clothes.

I've just returned from Cubi Point in the Philippines. That's where they send you after you've had twenty combat hops, after you are in the regimen of combat flying. I was there for eleven days learning how to take care of myself in case I get shot down. I learned how to get safe drinking water out of vines and how to gather, prepare, and cook wild rice (in a bamboo section) and how to find a place to sleep during the day where they can't find you. My job now is writing the daily flight schedule, plus flying daily. We get the "FRAG" (list of targets) from the air force telling us which targets to hit. Maintenance tells me how many airplanes are working. The operations board tells me which people are available to fly. I put it all together: Lieutenant X will fly airplane #000, taking off at 0 dark thirty to hit target #69. Of course I put down Grit, me and Randy, for the best hop every night. The writing and the flying works out to eighteen to twenty hours daily. Every fourth or fifth day, I get time to catch up on rest. Time flies. Months seem like weeks.

I thank you again for the nice letter that was waiting upon my return from the Philippines. There was also a letter from my mother. In it she told me, among other things, of the death of an old man in Piedmont. I was sorry to hear about Mister Bridge. He was a real southern gentleman and had a rare kind of poise I had always admired. My squadron has already lost two crews (four men) this year. When they don't come back, we mourn. But it was a different kind of mourning when I heard about Mister Bridge. He represented the South that I have always loved.

Now for the toughie: "Can it really be special with the right person, or is it just a romantic pipe dream? You are a man of the world. What do I need to know that will help me?" First of all, you have some invalid assumptions in your question. I am not a man of the world like you're talking about. Remember, I'm just a quiet boy who likes to fly jets. But during my brief college career, I read stuff I was interested in instead of studying what I was supposed to be studying, and one of the things I was interested in was the boy/girl stuff. Here's what I've come up with so far. The only job a boy has in his entire life is to spread his seed. The only job a girl has is to take care of the creature that comes from the seed. Spread seed, take care of the creature. The social significance of all that stuff and the daily application are up to you. Maybe you are supposed to wait for a "seed spreader" who you wouldn't mind being the daddy of your creature. Maybe you are supposed to try several seed spreaders so you are experienced and properly prepared when the right seed spreader comes along. I don't know how to judge from your perspective. I am, after all, a simple seed spreader. But you know how to judge. All you have to do is trust your judgment.

Okay, got to go fly. Thanks for the welcome-back-to-war letter that was waiting and for the peace I feel when I write to you.

Semper Fi,
Jay

April 16, 1968

Dear Mr. Seed Spreader,

Exams are coming up fast. I think I'll do pretty well, maybe even a three point six or three point eight. Everything seems to be falling into place, and I feel really prepared. I'm so much better at everything when I'm rested since I haven't had to search for a bed where it's quiet to sleep. Jena, my new roommate, is so calm and quiet, and she's always in bed by ten thirty or eleven. I try to be quiet if I come back to the room after she's asleep. Sometimes I feel like I'm the partier this semester. Glad you had a chance to rest a little in the Philippines. I can't imagine how tiring it must be to have to stay so focused.

Are you ready for another mission today? I am the enemy gunner! You have got to be kidding! The only spreading I'm aware of is horse manure, and I believe you are spreading it and not seeds. Perhaps in a more primitive time that was what folks had to be about in order to continue the human race, but I do think we have evolved a bit since then. Are you saying people have no value if they don't create a child, and women have no value if they never rear a child? What about those who never have children? What about those who never reach adulthood? What about Jesus Christ? What about grace? I have got to believe there is value in just being. I fear the heat and humidity are getting to you. You are an intelligent human being, a gifted pilot, and a wonderful letter writer. Surely you don't really believe what you just wrote. Where does love come in and romance and kisses and value just for being born?

My mother and my father were never affectionate in front of me. I only remember seeing them show affection once. Mama had a stove door that kept falling off. She finally began to prop it shut with a tobacco stick. One day I walked into the kitchen while Daddy was lying on the floor working on the oven door. He got up off the floor and began opening and closing the door. Whatever he had done caused the stove door to close, and it stayed shut. He then turned to Mother and said, "Kiss me quick, Martha, before the door falls off again." I was probably a high school freshman, and even at such an embarrassing age, this was one of the best memories I have of my parents. I definitely want this kind of comfortable affection in a life partner. Of course, I want it often, not once in a child's lifetime. I want someone who occasionally brings me flowers or leaves me sweet notes or calls for no reason. I mostly want someone who likes me for who I am. Someone who sees me as more than just a receptacle for his "seed" and a baby maker.

You never answered my question about my opportunities to be a Blue Angel. That's the heart of the issue I'm discussing when I'm dismissing your seed spreading BS. Even you, Matisse Rotha, my wonderful, fantastic fantasy pilot, don't see me for who I am. I have dreams and hopes and wants just like you. I want to be able to buy land in Arizona or fly the Grand Canyon, be an astronaut or shoot the moon or whatever. Give me a chance to be all I can be! As long as you and the rest of the world think my sole purpose is to have babies and rear them, I'll never reach my potential. No wonder women only got to vote forty-eight years ago. Talk about living in cages!

I'm sorry about Mr. Bridge. My great-uncle Euclid symbolizes that same southern gentleman as your Mr. Bridge. He is in his eighties. Ever since I was a little girl, he has made me feel important. He started teasing me the first time I ever met him, when I was about three. He asked me what my name was, and I told him, "My name is Ashley Beth." Without missing a beat, he said, "My name is Ashley Beth!" Since then we haven't missed a single interaction when we didn't argue over whose name was Ashley Beth. Uncle Euclid has a black couple living on his farm. They help take care of him. Charity cooks, cleans, and keeps his books. Jacob does odd jobs around his farm and drives Uncle Euclid wherever he needs to go. They are in their early seventies. Uncle Euclid has deeded them the plot of land with their house, and he splits his farm income with them. He also gives them money to donate to their church. They love him, and he loves them. This arrangement allows him to remain at home and to be independent. Uncle Euclid can barely see, but he keeps up with everything going on in the world. He talks fondly of my great-aunt who died a few years back. He delights in visits, and Mother and I go several times a year. I don't want to think about his inevitable death. There will be such a void in the world without his cheerful nature and wealth of stories. He remembers the eclipse of nineteen hundred. He says he was out in the field plowing, and the sky got dark, and the chickens went to roost, and they had no television or radios so no one knew what was happening. He let the mule out of his traces and ran back to the house fearful of what his father might say and the beating he would probably get. When he told his father about the mule, his father said, "Well, Son, if what happens is what I think might happen, it won't matter anyway." I need to take a tape recorder down there and capture some of his other stories, or they will be lost forever. Thanks for making me think of that.

If you're not too busy spreading your seed, write me. I enjoy the sparring, and I enjoy your letters. You make me think things through. When I talk to people, I'm just not as articulate.

Fondly,
Ashley Beth

22 April '68

Dear Alpha Bravo,

I'm not so sure how far we've evolved. I've just returned from two days in the boonies. The Seventh Marine Regiment needed some help calling in air strikes so, of course, they send Grit, me and Randy. A helicopter took us around to the various company and battalion locations. The helicopter pilot was this hotshot kid right out of flight school, flying a HU1E, "Huey," who insisted on flying right down in the rice paddies, literally with his skids right on top of the water in the rice paddies. There were Gooks out there working in the rice paddies that had to jump out of the way of the helicopter, but the copilot and the machine gunner and the other passenger seemed to think it was fine, so we zipped around from Da Nang to An Hoa to Chu Lai getting our briefings on infantry operations. Each location is called a firebase, and each firebase is on a big hill overlooking a lot of territory. The valleys and the bottoms of the hills are green and covered in vegetation, but the tops of the hills are red mud, clay, and dust, stripped of vegetation and covered in sandbags, barbed wire, big gun emplacements, and hundreds of people. They live in holes, elaborate tunnels, and caves they've dug in the red clay. Their food is brought in by helicopter; they send out patrols and shoot the big guns. We stayed at the firebases at night, in the holes in the ground. It was cool in there after the heat of the day, but in the middle of the night, the rats came. They were big rats; they got in all our stuff and crawled across us. The people who stayed there all the time didn't seem to mind. The next morning, we called in air strikes and went on a combat recon patrol with a squad of grunts. We went to a little ville, Thanh Binh, where the Viet Cong had attacked three days before and killed 114 civilians, mostly women, children, and old men. The people had been rebuilding with the help of a small group of marines. There were twelve marines there the night of the attack. Three were killed. All the others were wounded but fought on all night and saved Thanh Binh from total destruction. Walking through there yesterday, the only signs of a struggle were blotches of black soot, from the explosions, on the surviving thatched wooden buildings on stilts and the more permanent adobe-looking buildings, and the fresh stumps where trees were blown away, and the fresh graves. People were working yesterday. When they looked at us marching through their village, they seemed to be asking how far we've evolved. I'm not sure how far my seed spreader theory is from the truth. What we have here is definitely not campus life.

I'm so proud of you. You want to buy land—fly Grand Canyon—be an astronaut—shoot the moon. And, by the way, based on what you've said in all your letters, I would be the last person to think your sole purpose is to have babies. No, ma'am. Not you. I think you might want to get some things out of your system before you settle down, just like I did. Here's the deal: see it, want it, plan for it, work for it, have it. It's the American dream. And it really is blind to gender. Some people, including some women, try to skip some of the steps. They don't take time to see it clearly. They don't want it bad enough. They don't plan in great enough detail. They tire too easily. (In flight school, there were young cadets who really wanted to fly jets but couldn't concentrate on the proper method.) You can go from bright college student to Blue Angel or to anything else you want. And here's the deal with me: what I respect in another person is a sense of purpose and a maximum effort. If you know where you're headed, and you're trying hard, I'll like you, even if you are a girl.

My sixtieth mission is in a few hours. It is close air support—dive-bombing. We go out in a two-plane formation and are controlled by an airborne forward air controller, usually in an OV-10 observation aircraft. Dive-bombing is the only thing the A-4 and F-4 drivers do over here. It's fun but not as exciting as going into Laos at night close to the ground and running systems attacks, or going up north, downtown Hanoi, or hitting Haiphong with everybody shooting at you.

Right now I'm sitting here with Randy groovin' to the sounds of Money Makin' Merle Haggard who is singing his heart out about prisons and drunks and trains. I got several of Merle's tapes the last time I was in Thailand, and we like to sit here before we go fly and learn his songs so we can sing them while we fly.

The commandant dropped by a few days ago (just to see how I'm doing, of course) and said a bunch of marines will leave here soon, and the Marine Corps is going back to its peacetime mission of being deployed around the world, ready to invade any small, helpless nation at a moment's notice. So after my tour here, I can expect a tour on a carrier, maybe over near Europe or South America. I've never been there, so I might as well go see what it's like. Or I could get sent back to exotic Cherry Point. Anyhow, he said he will trim down the size of the Marine Corps, get rid of the undesirables and noncombatants, and keep only the small, elite group of trained killers who will make the marines the greatest fighting force in the world.

It's interesting how many of your stories remind me of people I've known. I wonder if we'd have ever met if we'd stayed in Larkinton and Piedmont.

Semper Fi,
Jay

April 27, 1968

Dear BS Spreader,

I was touched by your description of Thanh Binh. You posture such detachment, but reading between the lines ... well, it can't be easy. I'm so sorry. Did they attack because of the marines? Would their lives have been spared if the military presence were not in the village? Would those three marines still be alive? What kind of freedom will they have if we pull out? What kind of freedom will they have if we stay and hundreds more civilians and children are killed? Would it be better if we were not there? What is our fight about?

Your letter was welcome relief from the drudgery of finishing term papers, running for class senator, studying for finals, and biking tandem all over Parkville. It is always fun to see what your current implausible theory will be. You state you are "glad I bought into the seed spreader theory." My good marine, reread my letter!

You almost make me believe that being a woman isn't a detriment to accomplishing all those things I dream about. I like the idea of seeing it, wanting it, planning for it, working for it, and having it. That's what I did when I ran for class senator. I made this gigantic sign that several of my friends put up at the classroom building the morning of the election. No one could miss it as they walked to class. I won three-to-one over my opponent. I'm pretty independent. I decided early on not to join a sorority. I'm sure a lot of nice girls are in sororities, but once a person joins, it's like old friends are no longer significant. All the talk about sisterhood seems so cliquish and false. My opponent was in a fraternity. He thought the Greeks would support him just because they were brothers and sisters in this fraternal hogwash. I'll take my chances as an individual any day. I am me, and I don't fit any molds. I liked your line about liking me "even if you are a girl." I guess that's one of the things I like about you. You are in this awful situation, doing this awesome job very efficiently, but you're totally fifth grade and cute.

It's good to know Merle Haggard is flying with you. I'm not much of a country music fan, but if he keeps you safe, then by all means sing along with Merle. A lot of days when I come back to the room after class, and Jena is in a lab, I put the Righteous Brothers, the 5th Dimension, Peter, Paul and Mary, the Association, Bob Dylan, the Embers, or Joni Mitchell on my record player. Then I stretch out on the bed and unwind. Glen Campbell is probably as close as I get to country music. I like "By the Time I Get to Phoenix" and "Wichita Lineman." I love to dance and sing along. I can't play the guitar, but I plan to learn before I die. The Association always puts me in a particularly mellow mood, and I dream about my ideal man. Perhaps I'll put on "Cherish" today and think about what you are like.

Cherry Point ... sounds like we just might get to meet. I don't know if we would have met if we had stayed home in Piedmont and Larkinton. My birthday's in December, so I was four years behind you in school. Most high school students don't notice little kids, and that's all I would have been to you when you were in high school. (I went swimming in the pool in Piedmont once when I was twelve, now that I think about it.) I fell in love with someone your age when I was sixteen. He stayed in Larkinton for a summer with relatives and worked in the mill. He was a rising college junior, and I was a rising high school junior. At that time, the difference in age was too great. He went back to college, and I heard he married his high school sweetheart. I had it bad for a while. Since then, there hasn't been anyone who has taken my breath away like he did.

This semester I have been dating Mark, the guy who helped me get the job in Maine, but it's not the same as it was with Rich. How about you? Have you had many serious relationships? What makes a relationship serious for you? I guess our culture teaches girls to seek a romantic relationship, and my religion teaches me to wait for the right one. Is it possible to have romance in a long-term situation, or does it end with the "I do's," the dirty laundry, the dishes, the dirty house, and the screaming kids? I don't know why I'm asking you. I just write the things I think. I can hardly wait to hear your theory on this one. It must be fun coming up with all these theories. Perhaps your theories can be published when you get home! I'll keep copies, so you can compile them.

Uncle Euclid used to tell me about his cousin Henry who invented a flying machine. (Of course this was before the famous Wright Brothers' flight at Kitty Hawk.) Henry used to fly off the top of barns, and the neighbors called his contraption the turkey buzzard. Uncle Euclid said it looked sort of like a bicycle with wings that flapped. Inventiveness ran in the family, and even though the turkey buzzard never actually flew, the airplane inventor's brother Richard invented a machine gun that was patented and used worldwide (the Gatling gun). The airplane inventor was never successful, and his life ended early. I believe someone shot him while in the hog pen over some minor dispute. He may have been going hunting, and the gun discharged while he was feeding the hogs. I'm not sure what happened. I once asked Uncle Euclid if someone shot Henry in the hog pen. He said in his droll, dry way, "I think they shot him in the head." Thanks to the creativity of people like Henry and his brother, you have a job you love (flying planes). The machine gun invention probably helps the grunts as well as the enemy. By the way, I hated your description of the hotshot helicopter pilot who flew low to the ground just to make people jump out of the way. Inappropriate use of power is a terrible thing. I remember a particularly mean sixth-grade teacher who used to torture her students. She got away with it, too, just like your chopper guy. (Her husband came in and brought us Popsicles a couple of times that year. He knew what we were going through!)

It's time to go to the cafeteria. Annie likes to go early so we are the first in line. I don't know why she has this compulsion. She's skinny as a rail. We humor her and wait in line. It is fun to see everybody and talk.

Fondly,
Ashley Beth

PS: I wrote this poem after I received your last letter.

Juxtaposition
by Ashley Beth Justice

Bright sun streaming through
Newly minted spring leaves.
Singing birds, dancing squirrels,
Greening grass, warming winds;
God kisses the earth.

Shots ring out.
Birds fly startled.
In a ghetto, in a rice paddy, in a village,
Kisses only last an instant.

3 May '68

Dear Alpha Bravo,

When I was just a young child (last year), I used to wonder what it would be like to have a job and not have homework and just work and get paid. Now I know. Sunday is the only day that's different from any other because Sunday is when everybody takes malaria pills. We do cook steaks outside a couple of times a week, but it's hit or miss with the comings of the cargo plane from Australia. The cargo crew has cut a deal down under. I don't know what they're hauling down there, but they're bringing back steaks. I've flown eight times in seven days. I write the schedule every day. Randy is in charge of the fire control (electronics) shops. He does the paperwork and keeps the troops happy, and they keep all our magic boxes and computers and radar running. I've learned everything quickly here, and I've performed well under fire, especially going against the "Wall of Steel" over in Laos and going up north. The antiaircraft fire is intense, and the ol' heart beats fast every time I go there. But it's a good job. I'm pleased with the way things are going.

Thank you for the poem. I've never been into poetry just for the sake of poems, but I enjoy guitar and the old bluegrass and early country songs. It's not so much the playing of the guitar that draws me as it is the structure of the practicing and practicing and practicing. I like to get a song down good, so I practice a lot. And it doesn't really have to do with liking country music. Where I am now, doing what I'm doing, I come to live the country lyrics. Like Johnny Cash said in "Going to Memphis," "And when this levee's through, and I am too. Let the Honky Tonk roll on. By morning I'll be gone."

My other exposure to poetry came when I was at sea survival school in Okinawa. We had to learn how to survive if we punched out over water. We had to stay out in the ocean in our little one-man survival rafts for a day and a night. There were eight of us and an instructor in our little rafts, bobbing around with nothing to do but practice using the solar still and the shark repellent. We ate our survival food and prepared for dark. They told us to try to stay awake the first night in case rescue came. So this asshole air force cargo pilot decided to do us all a favor and recite limericks. It was a clear, calm night, no moon, only starlight, and every few minutes this asshole shouted out a limerick. He must have shouted 150 of them. By dawn we were all ready to shoot him with our flare pistols.

Your questions ("Would their lives have been spared? Why are we fighting here?") that prompted your poem "Juxtaposition" probably do have answers, but those answers are elusive. Fact is, we're here, and this is happening. It's not that I don't wonder about the answers. I'm just too busy to worry about them.

I had a girl who was my high school sweetheart. We went off to college together. I told her I had to go to war and fly jets, and I couldn't be with her. She married a cheerleader at college. The only relationship I have now is with my airplane. He has my name written on him, and I can count on him for my life. Now there's a basic relationship theory: marry someone you can count on for your life. (You always make fun of my implausible theories.) How about implausibility as a basis for a relationship? You should only love someone you can't count on, someone you don't believe. That way if they let you down, you're not disappointed. You didn't believe them anyhow. Then there's the heat theory: marry someone you can have hot sex with. If everything else goes to hell, at least you can have sex. And there's the friend theory: marry a friend, and if everything goes to hell, at least you still have a friend. Choose one.

Tell me more about this "senator" thing. Exactly what do you want to accomplish in this, your first elected office? Will you graduate to state politics, then to Washington? Do you want to conquer the universe?

And what the hell is fondly? You've been signing your letters "fondly." Is this an Emily Post thing? It sounds like something evil people do to little children. Can you really say "fondly" to a marine airplane driver? Well, you can choose your own closings. Just don't stop writing. You give me peace.

Semper Fi,
Jay

May 8, 1968

Dear Fondling Seed Spreader,

I'm having a heck of a time knowing how to close my letters to you. You with your affected and unoriginal "Semper Fi." "Always Faithful," always faithful to what? Me? The marines? Some girl you met in the Philippines? It's definitely a Matisse Rotha ending. (Secretly I kind of like it.) I tried "Keep safe," which didn't seem like enough. "Best regards" is for folks who don't know each other. "Love" is too intimate. (Heck, I don't even know if I like you.) "Like" is not a proper ending. I just don't know. How about "Warmly" this letter and "Affectionately" next letter? Or "Always?" What the heck does "Always" mean? "Sincerely?" "Yours truly?" Too businesslike. I'm truly always sincerely frustrated now.

I'm not sure I'll ever like a five-day or six-day-a-week job. I like and want to do so many different things, so settling down with one job will be hard for me. Take for instance my summer job last year when I worked as church secretary. One elderly gentleman used to delight in finding a grammatical error in the bulletin. What does it matter if I typed wisitors for visitors? Wouldn't it be pronounced that way if we were in Germany? And for the life of me, I can't understand why the preacher got so befuddled during the responsive reading. It just said monster instead of minister. He went right back to being a minister after that one line. Aren't we all monsters sometimes? For some reason, they haven't asked me back for next summer. (Thank you, God!)

Uncle Euclid is the only reason I ever liked to go fishing. He loves to fish. He is kind and funny, and I would go fishing just to hear his stories. He said he had a friend who had just been ordained and was scheduled to perform a baptism in the river the following Sunday. He asked my uncle if he could practice with him before the scheduled baptism. My uncle agreed, so they went into the river. Every time he would take my uncle under, the preacher would go through the whole spiel, "I baptize you in the name of the Father and the Son and the Holy Ghost." Now this preacher was a perfectionist, so he wound up dunking my uncle about thirty times. When they finally came to shore, two little boys had been seated on the bank watching the whole show. One of the boys looked up at the preacher and said, "He was a tough one, wasn't he, Preacher?" That's my favorite Bible story!

I have carefully studied your last three theories. First, love someone you can't count on so you won't be disappointed. Impossible: if you love them, you would be disappointed. This theory goes in file thirteen. Second is the heat theory. Good theory, but since I am inexperienced in thermostats out of control (I've been trained to control thermostats and to keep temperatures at a certain level until I marry), I cannot speak to the benefits of said theory. Third is the friend theory. Good theory but kind of like kissing your sister. Perhaps a combination of two and three, although I'm not so sure two and three combine very well. It would be sort of like a chemical experiment.

Of course I am going to run for public office one day. I want to be famous. To be famous, I either have to be a movie star, a ball player, or be elected to public office. I've been in a successful play, and now I have been elected a class senator. I played basketball in high school. All I have to do is choose which one will bring fame and money fastest. I guess I could also write a book, but I fear the publishers make most of the money. Perhaps I will write a book about elected office. Depending on which of your love theories I choose, the book could be either titillating or dull. If I am famous, the book will sell even if it isn't any good. Of course it will be good, if I can overcome my tendency toward errors on the typewriter.

Until the book writing begins, Jena, Annie, and I are sitting around thinking of country song titles to send to you. Here are a few:

- You can lock me up and throw away the key, but you can't keep my face from breaking out.
- My wife ran away with my best friend, and I sure do miss him.

Now you have to finish the song. Let your creative juices flow.

Warmly, keep safe, best regards, and fondly,
AB

13 May '68

Dear Alpha Bravo,

When I leave this place, I will fly my airplane across the ocean and land in California and fold my wings and ride around town until I find a burger. But before I continue my odyssey, before I do Vegas and fly the Grand Canyon and my new land, I will pause to name my airplane "Fondly." Fondly and I will fly over my new land. Then he will fold his wings and travel on the interstate toward Maine. Fondly is a boy because I ain't riding around the country with some girl. Me and Fondly will do adventurous things on the way to Maine. We'll stop by Nashville and record our new hit single, a love song that was suggested by our song advisory committee (you, Jena, and Annie):

Verse
My wife ran away
With my best friend.
I sure do miss him.
When we were together,
He'd fold his wings.
I'd kiss him.

Chorus
Fondly, Fondly,
I sure do miss my Fondly.
I should have known
He'd fly away.
I sure do miss my Fondly.

Refrain
I'll never get over my Fondly.

This past Friday I went out into the field again, this time to call in an air strike for the army down near Chu Lai. The strike was an A-6 leading two A-4s around with a total of thirty-eight five-hundred-pound bombs. They dropped about a mile from my position, and I was amazed at the noise and the shock waves. It must be a bad experience to have those things drop any closer. The people I was working with were at a fire-support base out in the middle of nowhere, some of the dirtiest, scruffiest people I've ever seen. Today I am exactly halfway through my tour over here. It doesn't seem like I've been here more than a couple of weeks. The time flies by. I've got ninety combat missions.

Johnson said forty thousand folks are going home soon, but there won't be any marines in the bunch. Every time the marines turn over an outpost or a town to the South Gook Army, the North Gooks take it away from them, but they won't attack a marine position anymore. So they want the grunts to stay at least until after next Tet. As long as the grunts are here, we'll fly for them. It's getting to where it's not as much fun. All of a sudden we're not getting shot at as much.

Everybody over here gets to go on R&R (rest and relaxation). We choose either Hong Kong, Bangkok, Sydney, or (for married personnel) Hawaii. I just got my orders for Sydney (my choice) for a whole week. It's coming at a good time. Everybody who goes there loves it, so I'll pack my Levis and boots and see what kind of trouble I can get into in Australia. Of course, Randy is going to Hawaii to meet Diane. So Randy is going through the "Not so fast, Mrs. Valovich" syndrome. That's the fear among the married men that they might get blown away on their last hop before their R&R and leave their widow stranded in Hawaii with a pile of insurance money. This all started with Lieutenant Val Valovich who refused to fly for three days before his R&R. The CO called Val in and asked him why he didn't want to fly. Val said, "I have this fear, sir, that my wife gets on a plane in Ohio. There must be about two hundred wives coming from there. They take off headed for Hawaii. After they take off, I get 'blowed away' over here. They fly on to Hawaii, land, two hundred wives get off the plane, and the authorities get them in a long, straight line, and say, 'Everybody whose husband is still alive, take one step forward. Not so fast, Mrs. Valovich.'"

I suggest you run for public office to achieve your fame. Ball players are generally a stupid lot, and being a movie star couldn't be fun with all those people hanging around and having to get all those divorces. But don't run for office just so you can write a book. You're supposed to want to save the world when you run for office, so if you are running just to be rich and famous, don't tell anybody. Or maybe you should tell everybody because it would be the truth. If you tell the truth, everybody will vote for you because people rarely hear the truth from political types. But if you tell the truth and get elected, you can't write the book because the book has to be about saving the world, and you just want to be rich and famous. The book can't be about being rich and famous, so you have to lie to get elected in order to save the world. I can see a place for me in your campaign organization. And, of course, Fondly will be there to help.

And now we must speak of love. As you can tell from my letters, I know nothing of it. We joke about the theories. You said in your last letter that "love" is too intimate a word to use in closing your letters. But your letters are full of love. Each letter is an act of love. Yours are the only love letters I've gotten since I've been at the war. So ... write me a love letter.

Semper Fi,
Jay

May 19, 1968

My Dearest Darling Pilot,

(How am I doing so far?)

My life has been so empty
Since you went away to war.
My body has such yearning
I may become a whore.
You took me to the mountaintop
And gave me oh such love.
And now I send you letters
On wings of a great white dove.
I love, love, love, love you.
I would not tell a lie.
You are my American hero,
My slice of apple pie.
The morning comes too quickly.
My bed is soft but cold.
If I do not see you soon,
I surely will grow old.
Oh come to me, my handsome prince.
Fly in your big steel bird.
Your presence is much better than
This paper and your word.

It's hard to write a love letter to someone who is going to Sydney for R&R without me. Have a great time. Travel is something else I want to do. I had a high school English teacher who went on the Queen Elizabeth II to Europe one summer. We would always get her to talk about the trip to get out of what we were doing in class. One day, Douglas, who always sat in the back of the class, kept cigarettes rolled up in his T-shirt, wore his hair slicked back, and paid attention only when the discussion had nothing to do with what we were studying, said, "Miss Spencer, how much did it cost to go on that trip?" Miss Spencer replied, "It cost twenty-five hundred dollars." Douglas responded incredulously, "You could have bought a new car!" I want to see Europe first, and then I want to see everywhere else. That's why I have to make money. That's why making money is more important than the issues.

We had an issue back during the student government election. You know, when I ran for class senator. The guy running for SGA president was in a fraternity (and you know what I think of fraternities). He wanted everybody to vote at the nearest place possible on campus. Now this campus is very small. The classroom building has been the only voting location since the college began electing student government officers. He wanted people to vote at the student union because his stupid fraternity brothers don't ever go to class. I couldn't believe folks who wanted to vote couldn't walk half the length of a football field. Having two locations doubles the number of poll workers. It creates the chance of double-voting because we are not assigned a place to vote. Well, I lost this one. Next election, we shall vote in the classroom building, in the student union, and in the post office. This is all because these guys can't get any farther than the post office or the student union on Election Day. I am contemplating dressing as Matisse Rotha, Wile E. Coyote, and myself to see if I can vote at all three places.

Please be careful. I end my correspondence with "keep safe" for a reason. Your letters make my day. I don't know what I would do if I couldn't write to my Flyboy. My Buddy from high school has been writing too. He is a medic on a helicopter. He talks about people dying as he works on them and rescuing them under heavy fire and firefights. I think he has a death wish because he is talking about going back for a second tour. Living on the edge must be scary and exciting at the same time. I've always wondered, and I still wonder, if this summer will be an exciting time for me. Will I have scary adventures this summer? Que sera.

Did I tell you I had an older brother who drowned? It happened a year and a half before I was born. My mother was in her forties when I was born, and his death is the only reason I am. I doubt they were thinking of having a baby at that age until he died. You know, I never thought of that until now, when I wrote it to you. Mother still tears up whenever she talks about him. He must have been wonderful. Everybody says he was just the best kid and the smartest. I wish I could have known him, but I probably wouldn't have been here if he had lived.

Mama said Daddy and my cousin were pulling stumps out of a pond he was building near the main highway that goes into Larkinton and on up to Richmond. My folks were going to build a new house behind this pond. My brother, who was nine, asked to go with Daddy. (Daddy always made us go ask Mama before we went off with him.) Mother let him go. He disappeared when my daddy and my cousin pulled a stump up the hill with the tractor. My cousin said they were only gone two or three minutes. When they returned, my brother was nowhere to be seen. Daddy began to dive in the pond. People began to stop to watch. My aunt and uncle had been visiting with Mother that day, and as they were going home, they saw the cars at the pond, found out my brother was missing, and went back to get Mother. They said she was making biscuits and came outside, hands covered in flour, saying, "You decided to stay for supper. I'm so glad." They told her my brother was missing and took her back to the pond.

College students from a nearby school came to help. Mother said these college students joined hands and walked across the pond, and that's how they found him. My cousin says they found him with a grappling hook near the shore where his tracks were last seen. Who knows how it really was? It was midnight before they pulled him out. Mother says she doesn't know how Daddy avoided falling into the water because he stepped from the dam into the boat as they brought my brother to shore. I think he disappeared around three o'clock.

Mama said they put my brother in the back of Daddy's car to take him uptown to the funeral home, but my cousin said they put him on the floorboard of the backseat of the police car. The police officer wasn't going to let my parents ride in the car, but Daddy had a fit, so they allowed Daddy and Mama to ride in the front seat. Mama says his hands were so wrinkled, and he felt so cold. My cousin who related how they found him said Mama couldn't understand why they put him on the floorboard of the backseat or why they just laid him on a table in the back of the funeral home in the little shorts he had on that day, all muddy and dirty from the pond, and the undertaker let people just walk back and see him. I don't know how it all fits, but I was born a year and a half later. Daddy never talked about it, and Mama mostly cries. She still does, and it's been nearly twenty-one years. I know it's why they have been so protective and strict. I try so hard to please them. I'll never be as smart or as good as he was. I'll never be him.

Enough about my wars! Let me end with a rip-roaring love note! You really are special to me. I feel close, as I said before. I think I would feel close if you were here. You try to sound hard and tough, but I sense you have a soft side, a side you don't show to many. Thanks for sharing it with me. You make me feel like I am smart and capable of doing whatever I want, as if it's okay to be a girl and not just a disappointment because I wasn't a boy. Because of that, I do love you and the letters you write. I don't know whether we would be an _item_ if you were near, but I would like to feel your presence and react to your nearness. (That's as far as I'm going with that. My thermostat is going haywire.) Keep safe.

Love,
Ashley Beth

24 May '68

Dear Alpha Bravo,

Australia came at a good time. I'm glad to be flying again. I really missed it. But the R&R made me remember how much I like people and pretty places, and it has had an effect on my attitude here. There are just too many places to see and too many good times to be had and too many people for me to meet to risk too much here. Sydney was nice, but it was too crowded, so I took a train to the little village of Katoomba in the Blue Mountains, a quaint place with a frontier-like appeal, like the American West but set in mountains similar to the Blue Ridge Mountains of North Carolina.

I drank beer and ate good food for a few days. The place was charming, and the beer was good. The only downer was losing my honky tater while I was gone. My sister sent me a sweet potato several months ago because she knows I like to put a sweet potato in a glass of water and watch it grow a vine. There was this old man back home that used to call sweet potatoes honky taters, so we all started calling sweet potatoes honky taters, and I named the one my sister sent to me honky tater, and I put it in a glass between my hooch and my bunker. It grew a beautiful vine, and while I was in Australia, one of them slimy communist gooners that works around the area stole it. They stole the only honky tater vine in Da Nang. They probably ate it. Aside from that, it was a great trip.

I've started a new job, Aircraft Division Officer, in charge of the engine, metal works, hydraulics, and ejection seat maintenance people. Their job is to keep the airplanes flying, and my job is to more or less hold things together and make sure the people keep busy. About eighty men are involved, and they work constantly with no days off and no "thank you." I'm trying to learn all I can about their work and do everything I can to solve their personal problems so they can concentrate on their work. It is more interesting and more challenging than what I was doing (writing the flight schedule and standing duty watch), although I did enjoy the other. They try to switch us junior officers around so we can get experience in several different jobs, and I requested this change. I want to learn as many different jobs as I can while I'm here, especially after seeing the chaos of the civilian world in Sydney. I had forgotten how unplanned everything is in the civilian world. It makes me want to sign up for a second tour over here, and I understand your chopper medic friend wanting another tour.

I'm sorry about your brother. You can't say the only reason you're here is to replace him. You've known of his death since you were little, but you've just begun to think of yourself as his replacement. This tells me you're at an age where it is normal to wonder how you relate to a bigger universe. Your world is suddenly bigger than Larkinton, and it's normal to wonder why you're here. I look at my own death every day, so I'm constantly trying to justify my existence. I'm constantly wondering why I'm alive. Sometimes the most convenient answer is not the right answer. "So I can die in the war" is my easiest answer. Some days I think it's true. Most of the time I think there's something past this war for me. Your easiest answer is you're here to replace your lost brother. You need to look for a more difficult answer. And remember, while your parents were protective, they were not protecting him, they were protecting you.

The controversy about voting places on campus was interesting and should be no surprise. You've got to figure that any boy who is in a fraternity is there because he's made an effort not to be here. Fraternity boys, draft dodgers, they're all the same. They, as you say, "can't walk half the length of a football field to vote," and they are too lazy to come over here. You watch them as you grow old. Remember who they are. They'll be too lazy to have a life; they'll be real estate developers and lawyers and shit like that.

I loved your poem. If you do become a whore, do you think you can find someone for Fondly? I'd hate to leave him alone in the parking lot while you and I get acquainted. And don't worry about your thermostat when you're writing me. Remember, wherever you are in your life right now, you can look straight down, and that's where I am. Straight through the earth, tucked safely as far away as I can be on the other side of the globe. You can tell me what you want to because you don't have to face me every day. I did, after all, have to raise two sisters. They were older than me, but I still had to do some raising of them. So I'm used to girl stuff. You need to be concentrating on your school work so you can get educated and run for something and conquer the world and write your book for the right reasons.

Semper Fi,
Jay

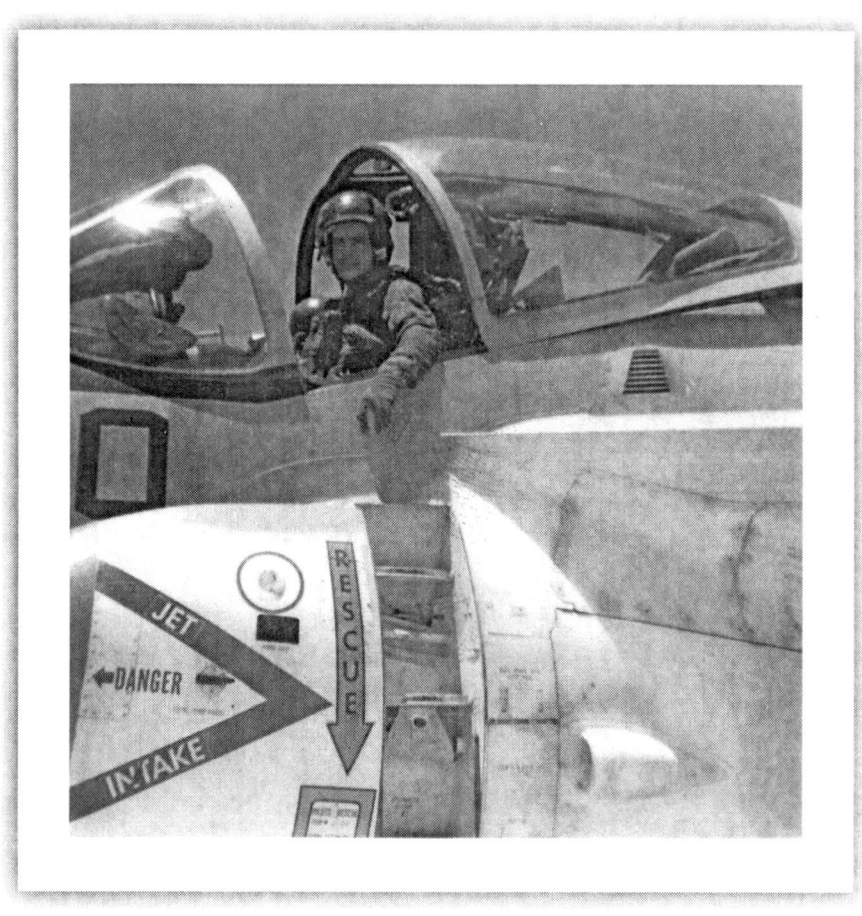

1st Lt. G. C. "Pete" Hendricks in his A-6 Intruder. The A-6 was capable of operating in all weather conditions to provide close and direct air support for ground elements of Allied Forces in the I Corps area of South Vietnam.

1st Lt. Hendricks preparing for takeoff from the Da Nang Air Base, Republic of Vietnam. Missions included attacking and destroying surface targets, day and night.

AD 640680

1653
10632

SECRET COMMANDO BOLT/AR BRIEF

MSN # *0956* CALL SIGN *MAN-74*

T/O *2330* ORD *22 D-2 YDC*

TGT *2400* CREW *Hendricks*

LAND *0100* A/C *CE-*

****

RINGNECK 325.0 *29.48* DNG *29.43* ABR ORBIT

RINGNECK MAINT 314.8 *1688* *225/43*

JOYRIDE 314.1/262.7/266.1 (c) 20 NM *255/44*
263.9

VICESQUAD 230.8/258.3/238.1 (c) 10 NM
out in

MOONBEAM 266.9/254.0/312.3 (c) 5 NM

INVERT 292.3/265.5/333.7 (c) BOMBS

COPPERHEAD 254.0/350.2/228.8 (c) ABORT

PANAMA 367.8/376.5/366.0 5 MIN BINGO

WOLF FAC 279.0 RECALL *MP*

H/K SUNLIT EXECUTE *KY*

HEADSHAD 276.5/356.0/325.5 (c) CNX *CNX*

MODE 1 *61* BORDER *YF*

MODE 3 *56* ARC LITE *EN*

PCZ *73* AUTH *Round Eyes*

NVN/DMZ *46* ON TARGET OFF

BASE LAT — HEAD — TIME *0700Z*

Ticket for a combat hop, which was clipped to the pilot's knee pad. It provided all available information a pilot needed to complete his mission successfully. Note the pencil changes made by the pilot to reflect the constantly changing circumstances.

Medals presented to Capt. Hendricks include (from left to right) the Distinguished Flying Cross Medal, the Air Medal (15 awards), the National Defense Medal, the Republic of Vietnam Service Medal, and the Vietnam Campaign Medal.

The Marine A-6 Intruder.

Entrance to 1st Lt. Hendricks' "hooch"—note the air conditioner. Pilots who flew at night had access to air conditioning so they could sleep during the heat of the day.

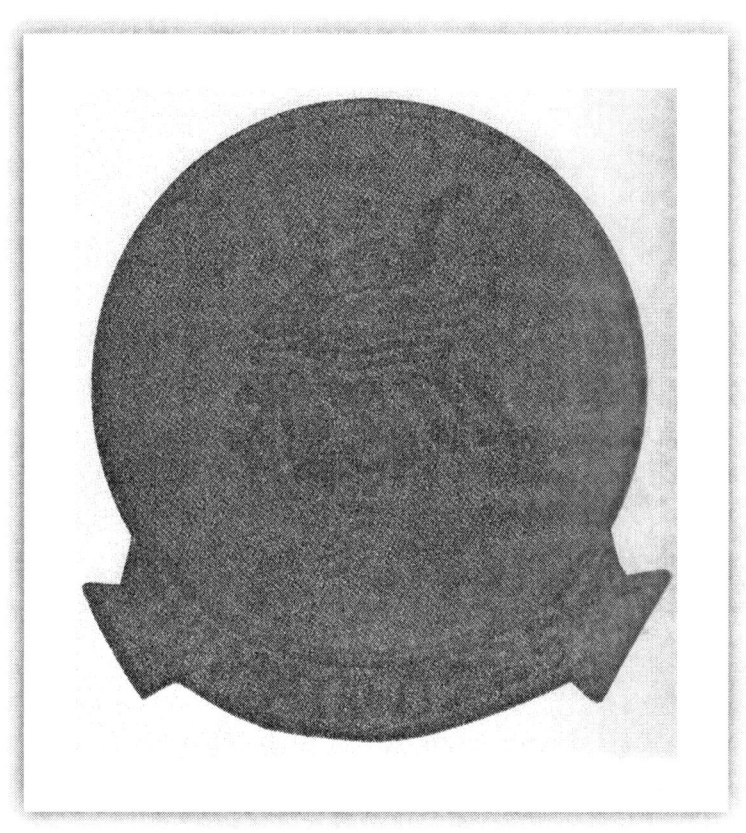

"Viking" insignia for the VMA (AW)–225 Squadron.

Flying over a military base near Saigon.

(The pictures from page 80 through page 99 were generously provided by Don W. Martin.)

Airplanes lined up at an air base near Saigon.

Company headquarters at a small air base.

Jeeps lined up outside the company headquarters.

A berm around the perimeter of an air-support base.

A lonely soldier thinking of home while sitting near two bomb shelters.

Radio and electronic equipment repairman SPC5 Don Martin.

An afternoon game of volleyball.

Bob Hope entertains the troops during a USO show at Long Binh Post.

The USO show draws a large crowd.

Pictures of Don Martin's squad members are displayed on the wall in a manner similar to Lt. Fox's description of pictures of fallen comrades hanging in the Officers' Club.

Burning off a little energy in a friendly game of football.

Playing football, a great way to pass the time.

Going long for a pass.

SPC5 Don Martin enjoys a little rest and relaxation time.

Someone must have said something funny.

A barge heading toward Saigon.

Sydney Harbor, Sydney, Australia—a popular R&R destination for many Vietnam soldiers.

Sydney Harbor Bridge.

A park in downtown Sydney.

May 29, 1968

Dear Honky Tater,

The ocean is just like that glass of water with that honky tater. I'm sitting here in a lawn chair letting the surf wash up over my feet that have rooted in the sand, getting deeper with each wave. The sun is warm and the breezes soft. My baby oil is on the shore, but my body glistens, and I'll probably sprout any minute now. Gosh it's great to kick back and relax. No exams. No papers. No more burning the midnight oil. I'm free! Me, Jena, Annie, and a couple of the guys we pass around are with us down at Jena's dad's beach house. He's down here too, with his boat. We've been skiing in the inland waterway. I got up on one ski on the second try. (This is to show you what a fine athlete I am.) I did fall during one of my skiing stints. Mr. Post had to push his little boat to get me up slalom, so we were literally flying. I hit the wake, flipped, and <u>pow</u>, I was in the water. I hit so hard it felt like my eyes were pushed back in my head. Today I'm beaching it, trying to grow roots and waiting for my eyes to move back into their sockets.

Your words about my brother made me think. First of all, I am definitely here to replace him. In my parents' minds, they needed a replacement to fill up the hole he left. The problem is I don't fit the same hole. The reason I came was to replace him; the reason I'm here may be different. If I didn't come to replace him, then why did he have to die? If I'm here for a different reason, why do I keep being put in the hole that doesn't fit? If my parents were protecting me, are they protecting me by keeping me in a hole that doesn't fit, or are they just trying to fill up the hole he left? You tell me, Mr. Down and Under the Center of the Earth so far away that you have to raise me like your sisters. (What the heck does that mean?) You should definitely be a philosopher because some of the ones I have studied don't make a lot of sense either. (By the way, one of my favorite movies is <u>Journey to the Center of the Earth</u>.)

Hey, get over this draft-dodger thing. I don't like the lazy guys who can't walk fifty yards to vote either, but they aren't the scourge of the earth. You made a conscious decision to be where you are. Some of them made a decision to be here. Some of them are even in ROTC. Some of them will follow you to Vietnam and die over there. You will come home and probably go back to school, and they will think you are lazy and good for nothing because you came home without finishing the job you were supposed to do. Quit whining, and quit the friendly fire. Save your wrath for the real enemies, the ones with the hydraulic guns and the ones inside your head who can't deal with the fact some people think differently than you.

I knew I shouldn't have put the word whore in the poem. I could have used bore or some other "or" sound, but no, I had to use whore. Now you are trying to make me find a used-up plane with dyed wings and too much paint to refuel Fondly. Well, I'm through writing poetry. The ramifications are just too great. Tell Fondly to find his own "or." He has such a hard-ass personality and ego, and I'll bet he's spit-shined all the time. Has he gotten a purple heart yet? Fondly is probably even jealous of me. I'll bet he secretly has a thing for you like you have for him. Well, I'm not wasting my time with Fondly. You and he have the special relationship, not me. Trust him. Depend on him, and I am sure he will bring you home safe, but the question is, will he keep you warm at night?

I think I should get out of the sun. Now I'm anthropomorphizing a plane. Not to mention that my pale, southern belle skin is tingly pink. I don't tan too well. Even when I have a great tan, I am lighter than most people. I don't usually burn too badly if I watch the time. It does feel great though to sit and watch the sea and hear the waves and lie on that blanket over there and nap. I didn't realize how tired I had gotten. Remember how I told you I like to dance? We've been going to the Pavilion every night and dancing for five hours straight. Sleeping late into the morning—well, as late as Annie will let us. She's one of these people who wants everything her way, and she has an opinion on everything. Now who else do I know who has a theory on everything? I can't remember his name. Many names seem to fit him.

Where's my love letter? I wrote you a poem and all this mushy-gushy stuff at the end. I even signed it love. Do I have to go back to signing my letters fondly? I liked your country song. Can't wait to hear you sing it. Send me a tape. Remember four things: love letter, country song, safety, and at least one more implausible theory.

Fondly affectionate,
AB

3 June '68

Dearest Alpha Bravo,
Love Letter:

Dearest darling, I pine for you. I yearn for your milky breasts. Not literally milky, they're just milky looking because they are pale and white ... I guess. Anyhow, the yearning makes my loins ache, and as you may or may not know, there's nothing worse than aching loins, especially when you're flying around in a jet, and you've got all that crap on anyhow, and it's all too tight, and you're hot because the cockpit really is uncomfortable and stinks. But I do pine for you, and I do yearn for you. As far as missing you goes, I can't really miss you because I've never met you, and until I meet you and have to leave you, I can't know whether I would miss you. Sorry. I imagine I would miss you. Maybe someday we will know. And I trust you. I trust you will write to me and make my day happy. So now, my dearest darling, I must go to fight again. I will return soon by mail.

All my love,
Honky Tater

Country Song: My git-fiddle got busted accidentally last night. Things got kinda rowdy around here after a few of the boys had too much whiskey. But we did manage to put together our new song called "Wall of Steel" and sung to the tune of "Ring of Fire."

If out west
You must fly,
You must be
Prepared to die.
Your ass will pucker,

And you will squeal
When you fly through
That wall of steel.

(Chorus)
We fly through that burning wall of steel.
And I'm telling you that shit is unreal.
And it booms, booms, booms,
That wall of steel,
That shit's unreal.

Safety: The flying is getting more interesting now. I've had several good missions in the last few days over across the fence (beyond the Wall of Steel), and it looks like things will be getting better with some new targets opening up. Our squadron has established itself as the most efficient one over here when it comes to taking out the hard targets. Of course Randy and I, Grit, have earned the reputation as the hottest crew in town. A tremendous amount of bombing is going on, but the Gooks keep rolling down the trail, so we get new targets all the time. Also under the heading of Safety, yesterday we got shot up a little, and the airplane wasn't flying right. We had forty fire trucks and two helicopters waiting to put out the fire if we screwed up the landing. About four miles out, with the landing gear malfunctioning and with the tension at its greatest, Randy said, "Hey, Grit." I said, "What?" He said, "I sho' do wish we was dove hunting in North Carolina right now." I remembered everything I had ever learned about flying and managed to catch the arresting gear with my tailhook on my only pass. Then, of course, everybody went to the bar because anybody who survives a crash gets to buy the whiskey. Later on was when my git-fiddle got busted.

Implausible Theory: Jay Fox theory of thermal

dynamics. Have you ever noticed, back there in the real world, how in September and October the leaves start to fall off the hardwoods? What you probably haven't noticed is at the same time the leaves start coming off, it starts getting cool, and the more leaves that fall, the colder it gets. My theory holds that leaves give off heat. When they are gone, it gets cold. When the leaves come back in the spring, it gets hot. I have studied this for years and believe it to be true. Tell me I'm wrong.

Now that I have fulfilled all your requirements for this letter, I can close by saying thank you for the great images you send. Sitting in the sand on the beach. Water skiing. Your tingly pink skin. Dancing all night. And by the way, tell Annie I love her.

Semper Fi,
Jay

June 8, 1968

Dear Git-fiddle Picker,

You are wrong. That's all I have to say about the leaf theory. You are wrong. You have always been wrong, and your next theory will probably be wrong too.

Careful with this stuff about milky breasts and other body parts. My mother used to say, "Don't write anything you wouldn't want your mother to read." It makes you seem crass and earthy—not my perfect fantasy. If we ever meet, you shall have a chance to implode my fantasy. But given that our experience with each other lacks touching, for God's sake keep the fantasy alive. Right now you are a white knight in shining armor with absolutely no vices. I too am this virginal maiden who has found her prince in the lush tropical jungles of Vietnam. My prince is a hero who only does good. He helps the poor and saves the helpless and destroys the evil menace that is taking over the country. He is always faithful (just as he signs his letters) to his beautiful letter-writing friend. He longs for her, but he would never crassly tell her he wants her body. That is his secret, and he will only share it when the two meet in a beautiful, green field and run into each other's arms. And then he will only take her when she is ready to be taken because he worships her and wants only what is in her best interest. (By the way, I am not quite ready yet.) If she is not quite ready, she would always resent his taking of her virtue, and their life together would never be the idyllic fantasy she has envisioned. He understands this because he is like <u>Father Knows Best</u> and always understands and has an answer for everything. She pours out her heart to him in her letters, telling him her dreams and hopes, all the while secretly wanting him to take care of her and meet all her needs so she won't have to always be achieving and making a name for herself playing basketball, being an actress, or running for elected office. In other words, cut the milky breasts stuff!

I've been home for three days. This summer is so different from last summer when death loomed in the distance. This summer screams of life and adventure. I have already packed a trunk to ship to Maine, and we will take it to the bus station tomorrow. My flight is scheduled for Friday the twelfth. I'm enclosing a card with my summer address. I do hope you will find it in your heart to write to me while I am in the cold northland. You can send me the warmth of the tropics since the summer in Maine is sweater weather most of the time. It's been eighty degrees here, and I am trying to keep my tan from last week's trip to the beach.

This time last summer, I had just graduated, Daddy was bedridden, and Mother was exhausted from the stress of taking care of a terminally ill person for the last year and a half. Someone had to be with him all the time, so I had to take over all the grocery shopping, collecting rent payments, and banking so Mother could stay home. I had worked in a small grocery store a couple of days a week after school and on Saturdays all through high school. The last day I worked at the store in beautiful downtown Larkinton was the night of the tournament finals in basketball (late February). Daddy was worse that day, so I had come home early from work to help Mother. Later that evening, my boss came by the house to see how Daddy was doing. He told me the coach had come by the store to let me know I had been chosen All-Conference. We had been eliminated earlier in the week, so not knowing about the award, I had not gone to the game.

Since it was already nine o'clock at night when I found out about the honor, I couldn't even get to the tournament finals in time to accept the award.

I wasn't the greatest basketball player, but I really hustled. I guess that's why I made All-Conference. I used to wear knee pads so I could slide across the floor for a loose ball before anyone else knew where it was. I played forward. My highest point total in a game was twelve. Foul shots were my specialty, and I used to get fouled a lot. I loved playing basketball. One day during practice, my pants split, so I tied a towel around my waist and continued playing. On class night, they gave me a towel. Getting the towel was comic relief, but missing the All-Conference Award presentation was one of the saddest days of my life.

I went by the high school the other day. That place where I used to feel so comfortable now feels strange. I don't fit anymore, and I don't even know all the teachers. All the things I thought were so important seem silly and young this year. I'm not sure I'll ever go there to visit again. Leaving home for one year has made me see things I never saw before. My life is in a different place. It's funny how things change in a year.

True story time. There was this girl named Marlene in my high school class. On class night, everyone went out to the trestle. I don't know what the fascination was for the trestle. Marlene, with two of my best buddies steadying her, decided to walk topless across the trestle. She is quite well endowed, and Rock and Joey have never recovered from their midnight trestle extravaganza. I missed the whole experience because I had to be home before it happened, but I almost think it was more fun to relive it through Rock's recounting of the experience. He embellishes it far more than the experience itself could have ever been. That's a lie! I wish I had been there, and I don't ever want to miss anything that momentous again.

Your country song is good, but remember my mother. You'll never get it published if she can't read it. I always listen to my mother. More important, keep safe when you burst through the Wall of Steel. You have made it this far. Don't get your name on some cross in Washington because you crashed into the wall. I really would like to meet you and not in a pine box. Never mind. I temporarily forgot you are a superhero, and nothing can ever happen to you. You just made up the landing gear problem, didn't you? I'm going to be so mad if anything happens to you before I get to meet you. I've invested a lot of time in writing letters, so you'd better come home and live up to my fantasy. <u>Just think about me for a change</u>. I will be devastated if I never get to meet Matisse Rotha. He is such a mysterious and handsome lieutenant fighter pilot. I also forbid you to become a POW. You must stay safe. Every day I want you to ask the question: "How can I stay safe, do my job, and come home to Ashley Beth?" Got that? It's your daily mantra. Even if we don't like each other when we meet, at least you will come home. One of the guys at school has a best friend from high school at the University of Georgia. His best friend's brother stepped on a land mine last week. He won't ever come home again. Don't you dare disappoint me!

I talked to Annie on the phone after I got your letter. She said, "Tell that Flyboy to go suck an egg." I'm afraid to say it, but I don't think she loves you. You'll have to get over her. Don't drown yourself in whiskey or do anything rash. In time she will just be another girl who is stubborn and only believes her own theories, and she'll probably become an airplane pilot. You'll manage somehow. As for me, I'm off to the Maine woods with its rocky coastline and its cold ocean to make my fortune or to marry some old millionaire who will "kick the bucket" on our wedding night, leaving me his stocks, bonds, and a cool million in cash.

Remember, no more landing gear foul-ups. Tell Fondly I saw a cute little piper cub the other day— petite, freshly painted, and new—and tell him he has to take care of you.

Always,
Ashley Beth

13 June '68

Dear Alpha Bravo,

Okay, I can't bash draft dodgers, I can't refer to body parts, and you were All-Conference in basketball, so you can probably whip my ass. This relationship, like all great institutions, is developing its own set of rules—rules that constantly limit freedom and restrict individuality. And I was shocked to learn that your fantasy person wants a fantasy boy partner to "take care of her and meet all her needs, so she won't have to always be achieving and making a name for herself." What? Where's the Cro-Magnon she-hunk who was going to conquer the universe in spite of all the gender discrimination in the way? You see, I've already conjured up a notion of returning from Viet Nam and running your campaigns as you conquer the universe. I want to use Fondly as the campaign bus. On evenings you don't have a sit-down banquet or a fundraiser, I'll cook us a couple of steaks on a little grill. I might drink a beer or two here or there. You'll be a rich widow by then. I'll be a roadie. So don't wimp out on me now, don't be a girl. I'll take care of all your needs. I'll drive your bus. It's the only postwar career plan I have.

You seem perplexed by the question: What will implode the fantasy when we really meet? I think it will be my little toes (I know you've outlawed body parts, but this is different). I just hope you don't see them until after I've taken you. I went to the beach with these people one time, and we were just sitting around, and this girl said, "Oh my God! What happened to your little toes?" and everybody looked at my toes. I didn't know anything had happened to my toes. They had always served me well. But all those people on the beach were laughing and pointing at my toes. One of them said I looked like the missing link between birds and man. I still don't know what's wrong with my toes, but if anything would implode your fantasy it might be them. So, like I say, you can't see my toes until after I've had you.

I was interested in your reaction to Larkinton after being away for a while, the new way you look at the town. Before I came over here, I did a lot of low-level flying out of Cherry Point. I liked to use Piedmont as a practice bombing target. I'd roll through there doing 550 knots right on the treetops. The town had always been just buildings and shade trees and streets and people going places, but flying low and fast, Piedmont is a blip on the radar and one church steeple sticking up out of a forest. The place is so small it doesn't even matter.

I've flown twenty hops in twenty-four days for a total of 107 combat missions. It looks like my goal of two hundred combat missions is within reason. I devote two or three hours each day to exercise and sunning my young body. The squadron has a basketball team, and I've enjoyed playing ball with these young troopers. I'm the only officer on the team. The others are younger than me, mostly black and from New York or Chicago. It's tough, earn-every-point street ball. It's hard for me to keep up with them, and I'm not as good as I was a few years ago in high school, but they think enough of me to let me play. The games are on a concrete pad that used to be a foundation of a building. A rocket came in one night and blew the building away. They cleared the rubbish and decided not to build another building on the concrete pad, and somebody hung a basketball net at each end. Pieces of steel are sticking up near half court, and where the rocket hit, the concrete is shattered and rough. It's hard to dribble because you don't know where the ball will bounce, and a fast break has to be all passing and no dribbling, but it's fun, and it's better than playing in the sand. We've got a big tournament coming up, and if we win, each of us gets an engraved Zippo lighter.

Da Nang was hit by rockets three nights ago. Randy and I were coming back from a combat hop about three in the morning. We had taken some shrapnel in the tail and had lost one of our two hydraulic systems. I had to shut down some hydraulic pumps to save the good system. We were a little low on fuel; twenty-seven hundred pounds is barely enough to make it to a divert base with a good airplane. We were about a mile from touchdown, coming in over the harbor, when all of Da Nang started to explode. I glanced at Randy. He studied the gauges and looked at the brilliant explosions on the runways and gave a thumbs-up. I raised the gear and flaps and went into a climb out on the 270-degree radial toward Ubon, Thailand. We could see the fires of Da Nang in our mirrors as we cruise-climbed over the mountains. We sat in silence for forty-three minutes, watching the fuel gauge and waiting for one of the remaining hydraulic pumps to fail, then shot a straight-in at Ubon and landed with two hundred pounds of fuel. I was scared shitless. I do not want to land in the jungle. You are either killed in the crash or taken prisoner, and I don't want either of those. But we made it, and it took two days to fix our airplane, so Grit has been sleeping and eating at the "O" Club and drinking a little bit of whiskey and waiting for a ride home for the last three days, over here in beautiful downtown Ubon. I've bought three suits and some slacks and shirts, tailor-made, high-quality silk and cotton, low prices, just what I need to hit the campaign trail—me, you, and Fondly.

Looks like we might get out of here today! They just told me the airplane is fixed, and the runways at Da Nang are operating. I kinda hate that I missed three hops in the last three days. I was trying to get thirty hops in thirty days when we got hit the other night. Oh well, I still have six months of flying left.

This might be the only letter you ever get from Ubon to Maine. Check out these cool Thai stamps on the envelope. I think the street scene on the one stamp is of downtown Ubon. I don't know who the man is on the other stamp. He's probably dead by now. They drive on the wrong side of the street here, so the taxi ride from the base into town the other night was as scary as getting shot and watching Da Nang explode and almost running out of fuel. Now I've got to take a taxi back out to the base, riding on the wrong side of the street, then strap sixty thousand pounds of metal and fuel on my back, and fly to Da Nang. I'm not sure I drank enough whiskey while I was here.

Tell Annie I love her.

Semper Fi,
Jay

June 18, 1968

My Dear Pilot,
   Your Thailand letter got here today, late afternoon. It was a welcome respite from the grunt cleaning and spiffing up being done to the Jordan Pond House. If one can be lower than the belly of a python in the jungle, that's where I have been. I arrived on the twelfth to find myself landing at a Quonset hut. It was the Bangor Airport. People were actually standing out on the runway waving at the plane. Now Raleigh-Durham is no international airport, but it is not a Quonset hut. And I have never seen folks out on the runways waving. Mark had driven up in late May, right after his graduation, so he picked me up. My first clue things weren't exactly right was when my luggage hadn't arrived. The bus station in Bar Harbor would not be open until Monday, so I couldn't check on my trunk. No suitcase, no trunk, no toothbrush, no deodorant, no clean underwear. There were only three other workers here, and the JPH was not habitable yet. We had to stay in a couple of rented rooms over a restaurant in Bar Harbor for one night until we cleaned the kitchen, dining rooms, and living quarters. The staff living quarters for the girls are over the kitchen. The guys are to live in a small house (they call it a cottage) out back of the restaurant. The other workers are arriving daily.
   It seems Mark forgot to tell me this Georgia peach named Collins had a thing for him the previous year. Of course she is one of the two girls who had arrived early. (I believe one of the others let it slip that Collins had ridden up with Mark, but they quickly tried to cover their tracks.) She is super thin, tall with dark hair and eyes. Has that finishing-girl smile like she

is holding a toothbrush between her teeth all the time. Of course being called by a family name is another giveaway. She looks daggers through me most of the time, and Mark just tries to act so cool like he doesn't have a clue.

To make matters worse, today when I walked into the kitchen, one of the guys from South Dakota had a giant moth hanging from the dishwasher with a sign around the moth's neck that read, "Don't Blow Martin." I walked over and blew Martin. Robby screamed out, "Ashley Beth just blew Martin." Sherry dropped a tray and doubled over laughing. Later she took me aside and explained my faux pas. I turned ten shades of crimson and backed out of the kitchen. I hate being made fun of, especially this way.

I have felt so homesick. I've never been homesick before in my life. I guess it's because I'm a thousand miles from home and can't go home. So far my expectations have not been met. Seven or eight more staffers arrived today. I have tried out several of the rooms over the kitchen and finally decided on one as far from Collins as possible. She is a hostess for the restaurant, and she sets the schedule, so she has arranged to have the same day off as Mark. I have the day off with two dorky girls and no guys. No one in my group has a car.

We have been practicing waitressing for the last two days. We have to carry all trays on our shoulders. We practiced with stones first. Did you know in order to prevent spilling a cup of coffee in a saucer you must carry it without looking at it? Try it sometime. We serve lunch at noon, tea and popovers on the lawn at four o'clock, and dinner from six to eight thirty. We serve finger bowls if folks have lobster. We can't write down what anyone orders. We have to remember it.

I'm glad the menu is limited. The restaurant opens on the twentieth, and we have a practice night on the nineteenth. We have free time in the mornings after we get our areas ready for lunch. Then we have a couple of hours after we serve lunch, and we are finished with dinner by eight thirty or nine at night. Several guys work in the kitchen and at the three gift shops in the Acadia National Park. A few local kids work here too. Just about every night, we go into Bar Harbor to dance at a disco.

I don't know where the "she-hunk Cro-Magnon" woman went. Right now she needs some taking care of. She hasn't even met her rich millionaire or made one single wedding plan. I need you and Fondly to get me through this. I called Mother and cried on the phone. I'm so afraid I won't make it. It's been cold and rainy, and I had to wear the same clothes for three days. (It's lucky I'm beautiful since I didn't have my makeup.) I don't feel very beautiful or clean or confident that my career as a politician will ever get off the ground. When I got my trunk and my luggage two days ago, I stood in the shower for thirty minutes, threw my overused clothes in the washer, and unpacked in my room that is far, far away from Miss Finishing School. Mark can have her.

So far my roommate hasn't arrived, but I expect her today. Can't you make a schedule that lets you fly to Maine tonight? Collins and Mark can go jump in the Jordan Pond for all I care. You would make a great impression on everyone. You could fly right between the Bubbles, two mountains that are on the far side of the Jordan Pond, and then land on the lawn. I could get one of the girls to practice serving you tea on the lawn. We could kiss and hug right in front of skinny Collins. Mark's old '61 Dodge Dart would look pathetic beside Fondly. I'm sure Fondly could find someone to hang out with at the Bangor Airport. He might even like the Quonset hut.

Your toes actually made me smile today, and I was pretty much determined to cry and look sad all day long. We must be related in the distant Neanderthal past. I have these mutant little toes. The other four toes look normal on each foot, but my little toes are so short there is hardly room for the nail to grow. It must be a sign. Just think when they find our footprints in the frozen tundra thousands of years from now, they will think we were aliens because our toes are so strange. I would prefer you don't stare at my feet when I first meet you, or you may turn and go the other way. I will try my best to avoid foot glances in your direction until we are settled on the campaign trail.

Your descriptions of flying and how powerful you feel are just great. I'm so envious. It must be the truest feeling of freedom to be above the earth, handling a jet filled with bombs, going vertical and then flipping upside down. How will you come down to earth when your tour is over? I don't think I would ever be satisfied with simply walking the earth if I had your experiences as a pilot. What can you possibly do that will be as exciting? My life is exactly the opposite. Everything I do is exciting because this is the first time I've ever done anything, and I've never been very far out of Larkinton until this summer. You've already been everywhere and done everything exciting, except meet me, of course! You must write your memoirs as you drive me down the campaign trail. Keeping the memories alive will be a great way to relive your exciting life.

Sorry you think my fantasies and our relationship are limiting our freedom and restricting our individuality. I would never do anything to hold you down. My life is freed by jumping into this fantasy. I guess it's the difference between being a girl and being a honky tater. My dreams are alive and well, but where is your honky tater?

I kissed the Thai stamps today. I needed to kiss someone, and you had touched them with your sweet lips. (It was definitely a poor substitute for the real thing, I guess.) It's sort of like holding your hand up to a window with someone else's hand pressed on the other side. I've always thought it would be a great scene in a movie where the girl is in a car that is slowly moving away. The guy is running along beside, both his hand and hers pressed together with only the glass between. I think I'll be a movie director. The hand on the window and kissing the stamps are nice touches. Don't you think? By the way, I don't like whiskey. Don't lick your stamps when you've been drinking. I have a very low tolerance for alcohol, and I've felt drunk ever since kissing those stamps.

How am I supposed to feel when you are always telling Annie you love her and you're just always faithful to me? I had a letter from Annie when I arrived here. She's working in an ink pen factory on an assembly line this summer. Last week she accidentally screwed her finger into the ink-pen top. I know it hurt, but when I read about it, it was hysterically funny. I can see her now walking around for the rest of her life with an ink pen screwed into her finger. I guess I could have worse jobs than hauling rocks around on trays at the Jordan Pond House.

Send me something I can keep forever from Vietnam. Something that will always remind me of you. A girl on my hall had this stone with the word Namaste carved in it. Her boyfriend sent it to her. Namaste means "I honor your spirit; I honor the light that is within you." Every time she touches it, she thinks of him and is reminded of what he thinks about her. I would like to feel this way about someone. I might even like to feel this way about you. I've written a poem to you using Namaste.

Namaste
by Ashley Beth Justice

Pounded by the sea,
Washed in salt and sand,
Wrapped in foam,
I tingle in the breezes that blow across your
    soul.
Warmed by the sun of your smile,
Caressed by the gentle winds of summer.
I cannot keep you.
You move back and forth
Crashing on the shore.
I stand sinking in crystal sands,
Thrilling to the depth of your spirit.
I see you in the horizon,
In the violet shimmers of sunset.
I cannot touch you,
Yet I know you are there.

Namaste,
Ashley Beth

23 June '68

Dear Alpha Bravo,

If I can't bash draft dodgers, then you can't be tacky. What is this "finishing-girl smile ... family name is another giveaway ... a room as far from Collins as possible ... Collins and Mark can go jump in the Jordan Pond for all I care"? Sounds like good ol'-fashioned southern country tackiness to me. Men have fought wars over the love of a woman. Men have squandered national fortunes. But no man has ever done anything that compares to the magnitude of the hatred and competition between two southern girls when some dumb young boy is at stake. I'm sure Mark is a nice boy, but it's not like you've promised your troth. And if you're going out dancing every night, things can't be so bad. You can dislike Collins, but you can't be tacky. You can't conquer the universe if you're tacky.

Thank you for the nice letter. You wrote it on my birthday, June 18. Flag Day is June 14, the day everybody flies their flags. My parents decided they would celebrate Flag Day on the eighteenth since I was supposed to be born the fourteenth but decided to wait a few days. Every year my father waits until the eighteenth to put out his flag in celebration of me.

Enclosed is a picture of ol' Jayray (my stage name) doing his rendition of "Detroit City" for the squadron. We had a USO show come through for a party in the hangar, and they made me get up and do my thing with the band. The red bandanna has flown every mission with me since you sent it, so it's right rank, but it's kept me alive, and it added a nice touch for my performance. The troops went nuts when I sang the chorus. Also enclosed is the picture of the basketball team right after we won the MAG-11 championship. We got our Zippo lighters, engraved:

CHAMPS
MAG-11
Da Nang
RVN
1968

I was disappointed to learn from your letter we will be unable to breed because of our common toe problem. We have to be responsible and remove this problem from the gene pool.

I'm sorry you're lonesome and homesick. I don't get that way here because this is such an exciting place, and there's no time for it. But I certainly remember the first time I was lonesome and homesick. I was an enlisted marine. I had finished a short enlisted training course at the Naval Air Station in Jacksonville, Florida. My orders to Officer Candidate School came through, but I had to wait a month before I could go, so they put me in a work pool. I spent all day cleaning shitters and cutting grass and trimming sidewalks. The work was so meticulous and so mundane, and what lay ahead—becoming an officer and maybe a pilot—was so full of promise and adventure, and I was so impatient. I decided to go to the enlisted club one Friday night. It was payday, and I was bored. I cleaned up and put on my civvies and started walking from the barracks to the club. It was about a mile on a straight sidewalk by an asphalt street. A big part of the mile was a swampy area where the street and sidewalk were on a dirt fill raised above the swamp. At the low point of the swamp was a culvert under the street. As I was walking near the culvert, I stopped and looked around. Almost dark, nobody around, even the birds had quit singing. And suddenly it came over me, that awful lonesome feeling. I started crying. I was shocked. I had never felt that way. Then I looked around to see if anybody was coming. I was a frigging marine, and I was standing there crying. I felt stupid, so I went down the bank and got in the culvert so nobody would see me. Of course once I was in the culvert, my sobbing amplified and echoed until I sounded like the monster in a B-grade Japanese horror flick. Then I realized if anybody walked by on the sidewalk up above and heard that awful noise, they would probably shoot first and ask questions later, so I started laughing then quit crying and went up to the sidewalk and to the club for a steak and some beer. But I'll never forget how lonesome and how homesick I was for a while. By now I'm sure you're all cleaned up and spiffy and cordial and efficient and, actually, quite happy. I know you're a good waitress. You just had a rough start in Maine.

We've started some serious bombing, so you might have to struggle through a summer in Maine without me and Fondly. Plans change here daily, and rumors surround all the changes, so it's hard to know what we'll be doing a month from now. I go through the Wall of Steel every night now. Randy and I don't talk anymore after we take off and climb out. We prepare ourselves for the antiaircraft fire, then we fly through it, then we hit our target. I lose a few pounds every time I fly, so I have to eat a lot of food. I think I mentioned in my first letter the enlisted cook down at the chow hall who cooks grits for Grit. One morning I told him how much energy I was burning every day, so he wrote to his mama in Alabama. She wrote back and said to "feed your cap'n like we'd feed on the farm." The enlisted cook at the chow hall has this theory: Find an animal with some fat on it and some fresh vegetables. Cook the animal. Use the meat broth to cook the vegetables. Make bread and plenty of it. All the cold, fresh milk you can drink. So our diet now is our grits and eggs in the morning at regular chow, when we get back from debriefing the night hop, before we go to sleep. Then we sleep and get up

June 28, 1968

Dear Zippo,

Your cold Zippo lighter warms quickly, and every time I'm lonely, I whip that lighter out and think of you. My tears are dried by the bright yellow flame that represents the light that is you and the light that is in you. Thank you. Your generous and unselfish gift is my most prized possession. It heightens my awareness of all that is good about this summer. It has even burned the tackiness from my pen. You shall never hear me refer to Collins negatively again. Can you ever forgive me? What can I say? I just wasn't myself.

There are about forty-five college students from all over the United States here for the summer. My roommate is from Ohio and goes to Pomona College in California. She is majoring in Russian. She lives in a dorm where they are only allowed to speak Russian. Next fall she is taking a year off and traveling around Europe. I really like her a lot, and I admire her spunk. She is very bright, and I am so glad I have the chance to room with her. Ruthie has dark, wavy hair and dark brown eyes. She wears scarves tied around her hair, and she looks like a gypsy, so traveling next fall across Europe will be easy for her. She and I have the same day off, and we have done a lot of hiking.

There is a restaurant in Bar Harbor named Martino's. They open in Bar Harbor in the summer and in Miami in the winter. I believe it is Mafia connected. The owner is this big, burly Italian gentleman who wears Armani suits, smokes Cuban cigars, and takes other "suited men" into a back room each night. He has this gorgeous blonde daughter who helps hostess. The staff goes with him to Florida in the winter. It's a pretty big operation. On my last day off, his daughter gave us a ride back to the JPH. She had met us several times when we came in for strawberry pie. I like her. She's so poised and lovely and treats everybody with respect. They are a mysterious family, though. We all speculate about their real business. I think I'll be a writer and make up this fantastic Mafia story about the Martinos. The food is great, not too expensive but somewhat elegant, especially for college students. When you get tired of Jordan Pond House food, we can run in to Bar Harbor to Martino's for their famous strawberry pie. You can help me speculate and write the outline for my novel. Maybe a story about a godfather and drugs and prostitution and restaurants as a cover. Naw ... who would want to read about that! Just don't become mesmerized by Julie Martino. It's not a good idea to get mixed up with the godfather's daughter.

I'm afraid the Quonset Slut is not located at the JPH but at the Bangor Airport. Fondly will have to leave you with me for a while and fly the sixty miles to Bangor alone.

Near here are beautiful homes built on cliffs overlooking the sea. We could pack a picnic lunch and park on one of those rocks, eat cheese and crackers, drink wine (or grape juice), and listen to the water pound the rocks. If the day is sunny, it will be comfortable to sun there in shorts, no jock straps allowed. You could bring your git-fiddle and play me a song. I'm so proud of your picture with the USO band. It must have been quite a high for you. We're going to do a variety/talent show this summer at the JPH.

Last Sunday I completed my morning duties and quickly changed into church clothes. Mr. Z, one of the managers, had told us he would personally take us to church if we wanted to go. Church starts at ten, so I knew I could be back in time for lunch. Two other girls went too. We went to a white-frame Congregationalist church. I was told it was very much like a Baptist church. It was very plain, inside and out, very New England, with a few squares of stained glass for color, not the pretty pictures we have in the windows at my home church. I knew I was in the wrong place when I saw kneeling benches. We also recited out of a prayer book and had to read various passages of the liturgy aloud. I couldn't find the correct reading, and I wound up being a frustrated worshipper. Why someone would say the Congregationalist church is like the Baptist church I grew up in is beyond me. They did not sing one stanza of "Just As I Am," and the town drunk didn't even go down to the front at the end of the service. Our ride was late, and I blew into the JPH five minutes before we had to serve lunch. I missed staff lunch, buttoned my waitress dress one button wrong all the way down, and was politely told by Mark to check my dress. Then my stomach growled while I was taking an order. I may try the Catholic church next. If I'm going to kneel, at least I'm going to do it on a padded bench, not one with splinters that run my hose, and if I can't find the proper place in the liturgy, it will be because it's in Latin, not English. I can at least confess my sins too, even if I don't understand the sermon. The most spiritual part of the day came at midafternoon when I walked down to the Bubbles and began this letter to you. I felt connected then.

Happy birthday a few days late! You are twenty-three. Is that right? My sister was twenty-three when she had her second child. I think I want to wait a few years before I marry, unless of course my millionaire sugar daddy comes along this summer.

Thank you for sharing your crying experience in

Jacksonville. You always seem so strong and sure of yourself. I like to know you can cry too. It makes me know there is tenderness in that strength, and that makes me like you better. I am okay now. There is much to do in the evenings and on my days off. I even manage to get in some hiking between morning chores and lunch. I thought I would miss the fast-food restaurants and the busyness of Raleigh, but now I am dreading going back to the hustle and bustle of school and everyday life. It's so quiet here, and there are trillions of stars in the sky at night that I never knew existed. And you have never seen a full moon until you have seen one rise over the Maine shoreline. It begins at the horizon as a gigantic, orange fireball. Slowly it moves up into the night sky until it sits in the heavens casting its glittering light on the water. It is a yellow sphere by then. When I watch it rise, I feel such peace. I have taken a memory snapshot that shall always be retrievable even if my eyes no longer work. I sometimes feel like I have walked into a little piece of heaven this summer. I'm sending lots of moonlight wishes and kisses to you. Look for them on your next moonlight mission. And don't worry about your heart. It's in my trunk, and unless my trunk gets lost on the return trip home, it will be waiting for you in North Carolina. I shall think of you at noon as I get ready to serve lunch and you leave for your combat mission.

I'm dropping the Beth from my name. I think Ashley sounds a bit more adult. What do you think?

Love,
Ashley

2 July '68

Dear Alpha,

Now that the Beth is gone, you are in charge. You are the Alpha female, and the Alpha female is always in charge. So is it time to begin the conquest of the world? Will Ruthie join our team? She speaks Russian, could run our counterespionage operations in Asia Major. It's obvious my first job as your campaign manager/bus driver will be to woo Julie Martino. I'll go to Martino's, and she'll see me and want me. I'll woo her. After we become close, I'll hit her up for a couple of million from her old man, to finance your campaign. What better financial backing than the Mafia. They always have lots of cash, they have good food at their gatherings, and their system of justice is very effective. It's the only funds we'll have to raise, and all I've got to do is not make Julie mad.

Things are the same here, flying every night, working out and eating heavy during the day. We have changed one thing over at the Officers' Club. That place was built of discarded plywood and packing crates and ammo boxes and anything else from the dump that was useful. But it has this nice covered patio where there's a little breeze in the evenings and some old folding chairs, and it's where they show a movie every night at eight o'clock. We used to get a new movie about every fourth night, so we'd watch the same movie for four nights, then change. But about two weeks ago, we got <u>Gone With the Wind</u>, and it's perfect for us. There are those love scenes, and Scarlett is so adorable, and there are good war scenes, but the best thing about GWTW is that it is real long. It has five reels of film, instead of two for a normal movie, and by the time they change reels and fix a couple of breaks, it takes four hours to show the movie. That puts us out at midnight, just in time to go to the flight line and start the preflight for our hop that night. Shorter movies leave us an hour or two between movie and flying to think about the flying. So we like the long movie and have decided to keep it and show it every night. We got tired of the same story every night, so we started rotating reels. Instead of watching reels one, two, three, four, five, we watch three, five, two, four, one. It's a different story that way. The South wins.

I'm a test pilot now. Every squadron has to have one to test the airplanes that have undergone major work. I have to take each plane out on a one-hour test profile before they can send it out on a combat mission. The test includes twenty minutes of acrobatics during which I press the engines and airframe to the limits of their performance curves. You can imagine the power one feels when you can move the stick and throttle and control what's up and what's down and the location of the earth. It's sheer power and pure freedom, and it was during my test hop late this afternoon when I wondered if I would ever meet you, and I decided I would meet you "after the fall." And these words came to me:

I shall see you after the fall,
Sometime after the frost;
After the vines are wilted
And the leaves are lost
To the crisp and lonely days
And the lonely, longer nights;
To the chaos and the beauty
Of one of God's great fights;
When snakes and bugs and stealthy things
Have crept and slid and crawled
To their hideouts in the woods,
And the cool of fall has called.

That was this evening. There's no movie tonight. The enlisted man who ran the projector got blown away last night in a rocket attack. The attacks are more frequent and come earlier in the evenings now, probably because there's no moon. When there's no moon, the Gooks in the mountains around Da Nang can come out of their caves and launch rockets into the airfield without being seen by the gunners on the helicopters who are looking for them. Out on our targets, we can fly low on a moonless night and not be seen by the antiaircraft crews. On the night of a full moon, those gun crews can actually hold our airplane in their sights as they bang away at us with their huge guns. So while your Maine moon is romantic and gorgeous, our moon is just something else to consider in the combat tactics being applied here. The moon here makes everything different.

I too tried going to church, thinking if all the church stuff is true, I might need some help while I'm here. The service was in the chow hall between breakfast and lunch. The cooks were in the back cooking, and dishes were clanging; there was no other music. The chaplain was impressive, plainspoken and believable. I think he's Presbyterian. About halfway through, I realized all the worshippers were new to this church stuff. Where were all the old-timers like me who have heard it all before? I guess by the time you get here, if you haven't personalized all the church stuff, it's too late.

I do like just Ashley. All the world is not "The South." You need only one name out here.

Semper Fi,
Jay

July 7, 1968

Dear Mr. Mafia Man,

I refuse to be mixed up in some drug cartel when I run for office and try to save the world. Just think of what I will have to promise if I get two million dollars from the Mafia. On top of that, I do not want you to woo Julie Martino. What am I supposed to do while you are wooing this stunning blonde whom I happen to like? I promised no more tackiness, and I am afraid I would slip back into old habits. I would have to hang out with Kip Dunlop, the Bar Harbor doctor's son who is quite handsome. He's already after me to go over to a deserted island with him and have a picnic one evening after work. When the tide is out, Kip says we can walk to the island and have a few hours before the sand passage is again covered with water. If we lose track of the time, we could be stuck there until the following day. Now you and I both know I'm not ready to lose track of time with Kip Dunlop on Barr Island.

A few days ago, several of us went up on top of Cadillac Mountain. We were determined to stay up all night to watch the sun rise. Cadillac Mountain is the first place in the United States where anyone can see the sunrise. We made a fire, cooked s'mores, and told ghost stories. I finally had my fill of chocolate in the wee hours of the morning of July Fourth. By four thirty, I could barely keep my eyes open. At 6:07 a.m. we had all rallied and were eager for the sunrise. During the night, a cloud cover had rolled in, and fog smothered the mountain, so this Independence Day the sun did not rise over Cadillac Mountain. I went back to the JPH and crawled into bed only to have Mrs. Tremain pounding on my door at eight thirty. She's the staff cook and lives upstairs with the girls. She was taking a trip to some craft show and July Fourth celebration and had invited me to go with her. I had the day off and had planned to go, but right then I could hardly see. We planned the Cadillac sunrise excursion on the spur of the moment. She was furious with me. Now, returning staffers made one thing quite clear: "Don't make Mrs. Tremain angry." I've been here less than a month, and the person who nurtures me with food is furious with me. I think I'll be a model. I'll probably be thin enough by fall.

Speaking of fall, I loved your poem. You truly amaze me sometimes. There's all this technical knowledge, and then in the midst of all the flight jargon, this poet rides through the heavens thinking of me. I know it is an exhilarating feeling to have power over the sky. You are wonderful, you know.

I read this poem the other day, and it made me think of you. I wish I had written it first. It's called "Love's Philosophy" by Percy Bysshe Shelley.

I

The fountains mingle with the river
And the rivers with the Ocean,
The winds of Heaven mix for ever
With a sweet emotion;
Nothing in the world is single;
All things by a law divine
In one spirit meet and mingle.
Why not I with thine?

II

See the mountains kiss high Heaven
And the waves clasp one another;
No sister-flower would be forgiven
If it disdained its brother;

And the sunlight clasps the earth
And the moonbeams kiss the sea;
What is all this sweet work worth
If thou kiss not me?

How can you stand it? Having people killed and hurt all around you. This war must end. I don't know who will be president in the fall since Johnson is no longer running, and Robert Kennedy was killed. You know he was killed in a kitchen just like where I work. Richard Nixon appears to be the front runner for the Republicans. Hubert Humphrey is picking up Kennedy's support in the Democratic Party. I hope whoever wins figures out a way to get us out of Vietnam. I used to see battlefields on television, and Vietnam seemed like some grade B movie. Now with you over there telling me the man who used to run the movies you watch each week was blown away ... it's just too scary. I know you are a great pilot, but you've also got to be lucky. Keep that sweaty bandanna. If it brings you luck, don't ever take it off. I'm also not sure I like you testing planes that have had major work done on them. Keep up with the time you're flying, and don't let the tide come in and maroon you with anyone but Fondly.

I too saw <u>Gone With the Wind</u> a few months back. I can't imagine watching it out of sequence. I would like to be able to write a historical novel like Margaret Mitchell did. She created some great characters. I get the feeling you might be a lot like Rhett Butler. I'm not quite as self-centered as Scarlett. Rhett certainly deserved better, although you have to admire Scarlett's spunk. She never seemed to see herself as doing anything wrong. There is one line from a Robert Burns poem I have always remembered. He wrote it after seeing lice crawling on the collar of a fancy lady in church. It went something like "Oh what a gi the gifties gi us to see ourselves as others see us."

Sometimes I'm truly surprised at how others see me. Just yesterday at lunch, someone at my table started to tell a dirty joke. He looked at me, stopped abruptly, and said, "I'll tell you later, when Ashley isn't here." The guy was trying not to offend me, or maybe he thought I wouldn't understand. I don't know whether I should be glad or offended that the staff can't be themselves around me. They all seem to like me, but I guess they see me as innocent. Why, I'm not as innocent as they think. I tasted a daiquiri at Martino's the other night. It really was quite good.

Tomorrow night we are going to cook lobsters in sea water at the beach. I've heard they are delicious cooked that way. We will melt butter so we can dip the meat. The beach we are going to is about a mile through the woods. We have to carry a big tin washtub, wood for the fire, lobsters, utensils for cracking, butter and pans for melting, beer, soft drinks, and ice chests. All this begins after the last person is served at the JPH. This beach is not sandy but rocky. I've hiked it in the daytime, but I've heard it is a whole new experience at night. I'll let you know if it lives up to my expectations. The entire staff is going. I'm glad, because a few of the kids seem to be left out sometimes.

I think of you often, and I try to remember to say a silent prayer for your safety whenever I think of you. Hi to Fondly and Randy.

Love,
Ashley

12 July '68

Dear Alpha,

> It may be even later
> Before I come to you.
> Maybe big, fat bugs will fly
> And frost will turn to dew.
> Maybe vines will start to wilt
> Again, as they have now.
> We never know! It can't be said!
> We never should allow
> Our minds to chase down hopes or dreams;
> Our souls to pause and pray.
> We can only stay the course
> And watch things crash our way.

I almost got nailed tonight. We had the two fifteen target time, and we're accustomed to it. We do it every night. But tonight was different. Fifteen miles from the target, at the southern end of the valley, we dropped to run-in altitude, down in the dark valley, and all at one time, at least a hundred guns came up. We always expect four or six guns at that point in the run, but tonight this huge barrage began. It was so bright Randy had to hide his eyes so he wouldn't lose his vision in the run, and the blast from the exploding artillery shells was bouncing us like a thunderstorm would. Randy had good radar, a good lock on our target, and those tracers and blowing shells kept sliding over the canopy. I just waited for a direct hit or for a wing to get blown off, but the airplane was humming, and Randy had a good target. We executed a good run. The barrage never stopped; there were new guns all along the mountain on both sides of the valley, and they were throwing up everything they had. Then we started getting tracked by some big guns we didn't even know were in the valley. The blasts from the big guns' shells were these huge, round balls of fire in front of us and to the sides, and coming out of each fireball were the fiery projectiles of hot steel. Some of them were orange or yellow, some were green, these huge, green blasts. We were flying through the lingering smoke from those blasts. Then we hit the target. The explosions kept going off all around, and the concussion waves kept throwing the airplane around. After twenty seconds, we were turning toward our climb out, and the whole valley started to explode. Our bombs touched off something, and the sides of the mountains and the valley floor exploded, and the blasts spread through the valley in an uneven pattern. We started feeling the shock waves from the blasts on the ground as we passed through six thousand feet. I was full power and max climb until we passed thirteen thousand, and Randy didn't think we'd been hit, so I just kept driving the airplane and looked around the sky, and I saw another airplane. The lights on the other airplane were blinking like they were supposed to, and I saw he was headed our way in the dark. I told Randy, and he called the controllers and asked if there were any other airplanes around. They said there were none. I looked at the other airplane, and it was closer and still headed our way, and I looked again and realized it was right on us and about to hit us, so I yanked the airplane inverted and told Randy to hang on, and the airplane went between us and the earth. It was so close when it passed that for an instant I could see the cockpit lights. I lost four thousand feet in an inverted dive, and when I righted myself, I realized the other plane almost hit us because I had forgotten to turn on my exterior lights after I left the target area. He never saw us. It was the first mistake I've ever made as a pilot, and we almost ran head-on into another airplane. I was not scared because of the blasts and the near-miss. I was scared because I forgot to turn my lights back on. I'm still scared. When I came back into the Ready Room after the hop, the duty officer took one look at me and said, "You're white as a sheet." So I've managed to get rid of most of the Jack Daniel's that was in our hooch. I'm telling you all this because I need to tell someone, and Randy already knows what happened tonight, and everybody else is asleep, and it's too early to go eat grits, and I ain't about to try to go to sleep because my eyes are wide open. So I have to tell you, and I've already decided to mail this when I finish it because you need to know this, and I need to tell somebody this. So I'll mail it no matter what.

Thank you for your letter. Here's my response. Don't be offended if people won't tell dirty jokes around you. It means they respect you. It's hard to earn respect, so consider it a compliment. And don't piss off the cook. (By the way, I had written the rest of the poem earlier. Just thought I would include it.)

Semper Fi,
Jay

PS: You mentioned Robert Kennedy getting shot. There wasn't much reaction here, but I remember the day his brother was shot. It was about noon when I heard the news that JFK was dead. My first thought was, "So Johnson finally gets to be king." I always thought Johnson had something to do with that murder.

July 17, 1968

Dear Crash and Burn,

Don't! Your last letter unnerved me. I take so many little things for granted. So many little things I can forget about, and it really doesn't matter. Just to think that you, Randy, and the other plane crew could have all been killed because you failed to turn on the lights. I can see why you couldn't sleep. Paste a little checklist in the cockpit with "Turn on the lights after a bombing run" highlighted. Remember you promised me you would "Keep safe." I don't want to receive your Blowed Away Box. I have no place for a rat skeleton, and the BBQ sauce just wouldn't be the same without you. As for the bandanna, if they can find it, the smell would be enough to ward off the flu. I've been thinking about sending you a box of my things. I think I'll call it my Goed Away Box, just in case I get marooned on the island with Kip Dunlop. It will contain my diary, which you will publish and get rich from the sale, my Vietnam Zippo (it wouldn't have meaning to anyone else), a tray with rocks on it, a piece of Martino's strawberry pie, and Martin the Moth with his sign still intact around his neck. I hope you never get my Goed Away Box because I sure as heck don't want yours. I would like the A-6 model and the git-fiddle as well as the Matisse Rotha play, but only if you hand them to me.

Last week, three of the strangest things happened. I know you are superstitious because you wear my red bandanna even though it must be rancid by now. What do you think these things mean? First, I had finished serving dinner, taken a shower, and was going on a date to the movies. My date had not yet arrived, so I walked out on the porch that surrounds the kitchen. Sometimes we serve tea and lunch there if the weather doesn't allow us on the lawn. Several staffers were sitting on the porch with candles as their only light. Three of them were kids who don't date or party very much. The fourth was my roommate, Ruthie. They huddled intensely around a large oval serving tray, which had been turned with the bottom of the tray facing up. The candles gave off an eerie glow as they flickered in the night. On the bottom of the tray, they had chalked in the letters of the alphabet, the words yes and no, and the numbers one through ten. A wine goblet was turned upside down, and each of the four placed a finger on the round part at the bottom of the stem of the goblet. They would ask a question, and the glass would move around the tray spelling a word or answering yes or no. Of course I was curious, so I sauntered over to find out what was happening. Ruthie was pleased to see me, but the other three were too intensely involved to notice, except that I was distracting Ruthie. One of the four asked the homemade Ouija board if I could stay. The goblet moved immediately to no. About that time, my date arrived, and we headed to the movies.

Second, the movie we saw was <u>Rosemary's Baby</u> starring Mia Farrow. I don't know whether you have heard of this movie, but it is about the devil impregnating Rosemary (Mia). It's sort of a reverse of Jesus's birth with all the pain and anguish that would accompany bearing the devil's child. Totally weird!

Finally, that same night I had the strangest dream. I was floating down a highway (it's the closest thing I can describe to an out-of-body experience). It was night, and I could see car lights passing right through me. I was at least two feet off the ground.

The road was a desolate country road. I floated off the road and entered a big white farmhouse similar to the one my family lived in until I was twelve. The front room had forties-style furniture, the kind that is stuffed, big and round and sort of like velvet but more bristly. The walls were green (my mother's favorite color). There was a fireplace, and there were hatboxes stacked beside the fireplace. This room was immaculate, very neat—the perfect forties' living room, like you might see in a Jimmy Stewart movie. I floated through a door on the other side of the room across from the front door. When I passed through the door, I was no longer floating, and the back of the house was in shambles. There were rough mountain people in the yard, and I was frightened. I managed to walk through the rubble of the house and across the cluttered yard without being noticed by these people. Once I got away from the house, I woke up. It was so real. I couldn't go back to sleep.

My thoughts. My brother died in the late forties. Before I was born, everything was in order. By the time I came into the world, everything had changed. I say this because I was out of body in the first part of the dream. When I went through the second door, everything was in shambles, and I was on the ground, no longer floating. Any thoughts? I'm not much at dream interpretation. Usually, I don't remember dreams. That's why this one was so significant. The best I can say is that I got away safely.

Back to the tray that told me I couldn't stay. Ruthie said they asked who was talking to them through the tray that night. A man's name was spelled out. The following day, two of them went to the library, and found his name with the help of the librarian, in a book on the history of Bar Harbor. It seems he had been killed while cutting down a tree for firewood. There was some question about his death. He was a man who had lived in the eighteen hundreds and is buried in the local cemetery. Ruthie was obviously spooked, and so was I. The dream, the movie, and the information about the man who died were too much for one night. None of the people participating were from the area, so none could have known about this character. I've never been much for superstitions, but all three things on the same night? Think back to July 12 or 13. Was anything happening with you that day? Were you in danger? This was happening between nine o'clock and midnight. The dream occurred sometime later in the night. It was still dark when I woke up. Your time is twelve hours different. Please don't make light of this. Is this the same day as your near crash? I'm almost afraid to hear your answer. I've never had so many weird coincidences occur on the same day. Do you think people are connected through thought? Annie and I used to talk about ideas like that. You know, <u>Twilight Zone</u> or <u>Outer Limits</u> ideas.

Write soon.

Love,
Ashley

22 July '68

Dear Alpha

On July 13, the airplane I almost ran into was in the wrong sector. I forgot my light. It was the same day you had your Ouija board experience, <u>Rosemary's Baby</u> movie, and dream. There is this thing called coincidence. There is stuff going on all over the world at the same time. Lots of different things happen at once. All it means is that there's stuff going on all over the world at the same time. It doesn't have to mean anything. The most interesting thing to me about your thirteenth of July is the man who died while cutting down a tree for firewood. Now there's a story, and I'll bet there are some great lessons to be learned from that man's life.

Dream interpretation: your room is neat, and the next girl down the hall is a slob, and the day before your dream, you saw her room, and on the way to the store, you saw a house like you used to live in, and that night, in your dream, you reviewed your day, and those two things got welded somehow into your dream. Dreams don't have to mean anything—it's what the second verse of my poem was about in my last letter. Dreams are images over which we have no control. You need to read the Old Testament. Remember, you are the ultimate conquest for some young stud. You are unspoiled, unbothered. So if you get marooned on the island with Kip Dunlop, he will be after the prize: your innocence. So if he's hustling you, make sure you're hustling him too. After all, campaign finance is our number-one priority. We've got to have something to do when all this is over. Maybe your job in the campaign to conquer the universe is slightly different from what we had first envisioned. Maybe you have to woo the Dunlops of the world to finance the campaign. And by the way, if we get elected, you know, at the universe level, like we're in charge, exactly what is it we are going to do? Should I begin my epic work: Rayjay's Rules of the Universe, which will, of course, someday, replace the Bible. I don't know. Seems like a mighty big job. Maybe I'll just fly crop dusters or drop slurry on forest fires. Maybe I'll stay in the Marine Corps. You could come see me, and we would decide not to conquer the universe, it's too much work. Then we could walk hand in hand and sing while the little biddy deer run blithely through the meadow. Then we could settle down in a small southern town and be superficial assholes. So ... I dunno.

I don't make light of your thoughts. I don't believe linking the events of the thirteenth of July is a bad thing to do. Maybe there is some grand plan that's made in heaven, and peoples' destinies are scripted. Maybe the Greeks were right; big gods look down on little man, at the drama and the absurdity of it all. All I know for sure is I'm glad I had you to write to the morning of July 13. Anything you can do to explain to me how you happened to be there, I will accept. I don't care how you got there. I'm flying safer now because of you, and I thank you for that.

Semper Fi,
Jay

July 27, 1968

Dear Mr. Answer for Everything,

You're about as romantic as a stump. I choose to think we are connected, and all those things that occurred on July 12 and 13 were a result of our connectedness. By the way, how did the goblet spell out that name? And how did there happen to be a real person who was named whatever the heck his name was who happened to live near Bar Harbor? I also happen to think dreams do mean something. I just don't know exactly what. If there ever was an ounce of romanticism in you, dig deep, find it again. Don't let this awful war take that completely away from you. Sometimes I believe you are twenty-three going on fifty. Well, I'm not ever going to grow old. It's just not worth it if I have to give up romance and dreams. I'm writing to you because you needed me to write to you. Maybe I needed you to write to me too.

My current fling is Charles Patrick, a true southern gentleman who attends the University of the South. More importantly, he has a car and the same day off I do. We are no longer hiking around the Bubbles. We are traveling! I heard a great country song the other day. It went something like this: "I love you honey, I love your money, but most of all I love your automobile!" Now I can really relate to that song. Kip Dunlop is in the past. I never did lose track of time on that island, no matter how hard he tried to distract me. It was a fun night, though. Just think of being on a deserted island. Every day is a new adventure.

Night before last, after the last customer was served, the dining room was cleaned, and everyone had changed into comfortable clothes, we celebrated Christmas. We decided that since none of us would be together at Christmas, we would celebrate it on July

25. We got a tree, strung popcorn, made ornaments, and bought or made gag gifts earlier in the week. All the preparation added to the excitement. We sang Christmas carols, ate goodies, and exchanged our gifts. It was great fun, and I really felt closer to some of the staff than I had before. Next week we will celebrate New Year's. I think we'll do our celebrating out on the beach with another lobster feast. Just to think I had never ever tried lobster until this summer. Don't you think it's a great way to spend New Year's?

We're also planning a talent show for early August. Robby, the dishwasher, and I are going to sing a song from <u>My Fair Lady</u>. I'm going to dress up as Liza Doolittle, and we will sing "Wouldn't It Be Lov-er-ly" in parts. He's a better singer than I am, but I've been practicing my singing voice with a Cockney accent. I've never been brave enough to sing in public before, so this is a real stretch for me. I love doing it. I know I can do it if I try. Perhaps you and I can become a singing duo if the political scene doesn't materialize. You've already had your moment on the stage with the USO show, but you can drive the bus, play the git-fiddle, cook the steaks, and write country music while we tour. I'll be a diva who sleeps until noon and is waited on hand and foot (just don't look at my little toes). Every night will be a new town with sold-out auditoriums. Our fame will spread far and wide. Now that I think about it, it may be more fun than ruling the universe. I'm very tolerant of people who are different, so it would be hard for me to make rules for other people. If we choose the political route, you may have to be my speech writer and make up new laws for my subjects. It's so hard to pick a future when the whole world is waiting for us. I just can't decide. Maybe the new year will bring the answers. I can tell you right now, I'll never settle down in a small southern town and be superficial. It just isn't me!

A few nights ago, about ten of us went into Bar Harbor to dance at the disco. Everybody had been drinking (except me), so I was picked to drive Mark's car. I'm not sure who drove the other car. As luck would have it, the ranger thought we were making a little too much noise at midnight. I had never driven a straight-gear car, so my contribution to the noise problem was bucking and backfiring his little Dodge. Mark pitched about ten beer cans out of the car just prior to our stop with the ranger. He began to question me, and I honestly told him I hadn't been drinking. The second car pulled up behind us, and Delores jumped out, staggered up to the ranger, and started giving him down the country. She swaggered, "I'll have you know Ashley doesn't drink. You just go ask anyone at the JPH. They'll tell you." She slipped on the side of the road and fell back into the other car. The ranger wasn't a whole lot older than we were. After a warning not to make so much noise, he let us go. For some reason, he hadn't seen Mark throw out the cans. The next morning, the manager of the JPH made slight mention of an incident with the ranger. None of us volunteered any extra information. Why, we were as innocent as little lambs, little lambs with hangovers, especially Delores.

What is it with this Semper Fi-ing me again? I thought a big bad marine pilot could be more creative.

Fondly,
Ashley

1 August '68

Dear Alpha,

Okay. Okay. Okay! I don't believe "this awful war is taking romanticism completely away from me." First of all, it ain't that bad for me here. I eat good, run three miles every day, and drink my favorite whiskey. And I get to drive the greatest air machine ever built by man through intense enemy fire every night. It don't get any better for a boy who's no longer a kid. I like what I'm doing, and I'm good at it. But it is all-consuming. Romantic notions take time. I just don't have the time. The notion is there. I'll send it to you in my every letter. Sure, there's a pattern to all this. But why waste time figuring out why? I'd rather just write the letter today, get a letter from you tomorrow, and not worry about why.

You sound happy. In one of my early letters, I mentioned how you might bond with folks there and get some esprit de corps and really enjoy the group effort. I'm sure everybody is trying hard in the operation of JPH—the old work hard and play hard trick. And your dizzying dating schedule! Isn't it funny how they get your attention and the pleasure of your company and your charm and your smiles, but it's me, way over here, who gets your innocence once a week, on paper. It's what we're all after, and you chose me. So maybe it's time to start planning our first union, the first time I get your attention and the pleasure of your company. I don't know when it will be because of the uncertainty surrounding my job. But it sure would be nice if we could start setting something up for late fall, after you're back at school. We might be through over here by then.

The Officers' Club is this big pile of ammo crates, scrap lumber, and metal roofing put together by people in their spare time. The big barroom inside is not too bad a room.

They sealed all the holes in the walls and painted the ceiling and hung the squadron plaques and pictures of all the dead guys. It's a nice bar. The beer is cold, and the whiskey is not watered down. Most of us are flying every night, so we've started going to the club about 0500 every morning, just as the sun is coming up. We have a few cold beers fast then start on the whiskey. Then we have the skit, one each morning, rotating among the five squadrons, so every fifth morning my squadron puts on a skit, usually about flying, usually a couple of lieutenants in folding chairs acting like they're flying around not knowing what they're doing, and then along comes a colonel and saves the day. It's mostly vaudevillian jokes and exaggerated facial expressions, but sometimes we'll actually have a plot and some drama. There's always a song. The morning skits are getting more popular, and the more people who come, the more fun they are. We're starting to use makeup, and some of the officers sent letters to their mothers asking for old dresses for costumes for the inevitable damsels who show up in distress.

News from Piedmont is relatively bland. My parents send copies of the local weekly newspaper. You would think all this over here is not even going on. Aunt Sally visits Uncle Joe on Sunday, the swimming pool has been crowded, somebody lost a dog. There were several brides last month, the town board can't agree on what color to paint the courtroom. It's hard to imagine going back there. Those poor people aren't doing anything.

I like the idea of starting a singing group back there in the real world. Since I started writing to you, I've also started writing some songs and poems, and they come to me at the strangest times, like when I'm in the middle of a bomb run, or when we go to breakfast after the skits. I try to jot down the lines as they come to me, because if I don't write them down I'll forget them. I've started playing the git-fiddle when I wake up in the afternoon, before I go to the sixteen hundred brief and get my target assignment. I'm usually rested in the afternoon, and my mind is clear. I'll send them as they're finished.

Love,
Jay

August 6, 1968

Dear Jayray,

Daddy died one year ago yesterday. My aunt and sister were spending the night at the house. My cousin's husband was sitting with Daddy so Mother could get some rest. Mother was sleeping with me in the bedroom across the hall from Daddy. Len called us to come quickly. He said he thought Daddy was dying. When we got in the room, Daddy was already gone. His mouth was open, and there was great pain and fear on his face. His eyes were like deep, dark pools staring up at the ceiling. I've always heard death is peaceful, but I don't believe it. He looked so afraid. I hope he's not afraid now. I couldn't cry. I did most of my crying a year and a half earlier when we found out he had cancer. From that point on, there were gifts of hope when he would try a new medication or go through an operation, but for the last six months of his life, there was no hope, only great pain and suffering.

Two men used to come to the house twice a day to take him to the bathroom. Mother learned how to give him injections of morphine for pain. The doctor would come out about once a week. The local barber would come out once a month and cut his hair, free. The wife of one of the men Daddy fox hunted with would make us a big pot of soup every two weeks. The other week she would make us a coconut cake. She did this for six months, maybe longer. A lot of people would say, "If there is anything we can do, let us know." But they didn't mean it. If they had meant it, they would have just done something like the soup lady did, and the barber, and the two men who came to help. One of Daddy's best friends would ask what he could do. Mother would say, "Just come and sit with him and talk." Mr. George would say, "I just can't stand to see him like he is." I learned a lot those two years. I missed a lot my senior year. I'm still learning a lot this summer in Maine, and I'm not missing anything.

My waitress partner's mother died last summer too. We've talked about the similarity of our experiences. The difference is this—she's been in a grand funk for the last week. Somehow she thinks she must be mournful for at least a week on the anniversary of her mother's death. I have tried to avoid thinking about Daddy's death until looking at the calendar reminded me. There's nothing a mournful nature can do to bring him back. There was nothing I could do when he was so sick except wait on him and help him. Nothing ever made him better, and he was in such pain. I'm glad he died when he did. I couldn't bear to watch him suffer any longer. If that is crass and callous, then it's who I am.

Yesterday I served a man who sat alone. He asked me about my school and home, and he shared that he had a daughter working in Florida. Usually a party of one is a downer because the time spent serving equals a paltry tip. Not this guy. He left a twenty-dollar tip! I think Daddy sent him to me just when I needed him. (Did I tell you someone saw a light over our house going straight up to heaven the night Daddy died?)

Two nights ago, four of us hiked up to the ruins. There was a great fire in Bar Harbor during the forties. Some of the people who were burned out just moved away, never rebuilt, and all that is left are the ruins of mansions that hosted great parties. Naturally, we never saw the No Trespassing signs. The place we visited had a turret above a guest house that served as a changing room for the pool. It was still pretty much intact. A column or two remained where the house had stood, but the most fascinating ruin was the pool, a huge Olympic-size pool. On the sides of the pool were portholes and a hallway so people could walk around the edges of the pool underground and watch the swimmers through the portholes. Of course we walked everywhere we could. I could almost hear the splashing and the laughter and the music coming from the lawn. I could see myself partying, flirting, and diving into the pool. Perhaps Annie is right, and there are past lives. It's fun to think about.

Last week it was actually hot enough to go swimming at a lake after work. We can't swim in the Jordan Pond because it is a water source, but we can go to Echo Lake (about thirty miles from here) to swim. We dived in from the sides of cliffs. It was refreshingly cool but not so cold that I couldn't stand it like my experience with the ocean in Maine. I walked out in Seal Harbor one day, and the water covered my feet and ankles. I immediately turned around and walked out of the icy cold water. My feet and ankles were blue. One girl who hails from Michigan goes swimming at Sandy Beach near Thunder Hole. I haven't been brave enough to venture past my knees (I fear cardiac arrest). She swims out to the buoys and bobs around just like a buoy for hours. She's a bit on the heavy side, so her extra layer of skin plus her Michigan heritage make swimming in the cold water a piece of cake. For me, I think I need a wet suit.

Take care.

Love,
Ashley

PS: Your Officers' Club sounds like fun. I'm looking forward to going on the road with you. My chances of being a young widow are fleeting. I hear all the sugar daddies have gone to Nantucket this summer. The talent show is three days away.

11 August '68

Dear Alpha,

Death is all around me here. Everything here has to do with death. The machines are machines of death. The meals are meals for the dead. Then I hear of death there too—your father, Mister Bridge, your partner's mom. Death here is different from death there. Death of young people is different from death of old people. When a country says, "We're willing to send our young people to die to prove our point," then the other country says, "We'll speed up death in our country too, because we believe we are right and should prevail." Then death is sped up on the battlefield, and eventually one side can no longer tolerate speeding up death among her young citizenry, and the conflict is settled, and both sides go back to dying of old age. Your father's death was a hard one, but he did have a chance to produce you and do some farming. I have an idea those were his passions, and from my point of view, here now, his way of passing is very attractive. But I hear your cries about what was taken from your life while he was dying.

Monday
by Jay Fox

The first day after Sunday has got to be the best.
My mind is filled with plans and dreams; my body's filled
    with rest.

Tuesday morn I woke up soon and plowed the bottom up,
Shot a rabbit, played a tune, my bitch dog had six pups.
That afternoon I chopped some wood; a flock of geese
    went by.
The sunset blazed, the moon was full in the cool, crisp
    autumn sky.

Wednesday was a real big day—I took some pigs to town.
Bought a steak, a mess of greens, a beer to wash it down.
Got some boots, hardware and flour, a tank of gas and
  stuff,
And wanted a pretty shirt they had but figured I'd bought
  enough.

The next three days were long and hard, mending fence
  and such.
By Saturday night my back was sore—didn't feel like very
  much.
I sat in the kitchen, looked around, and ate a homemade
  stew,
Read a book, poked up the fire, and mostly thought of you.

Sunday mornin' I'z feeling blue and went out in the yard.
I knew my life was like my land; they both were cold and
  hard.
I thought of God and happiness and heaven up above,
And knew that what I want the most is you and kids and
  love.

That first day after Sunday has got to be the best.
My mind is filled with plans and dreams; my body's filled
  with rest.

As you can imagine, there are ruins here too. We've
started flying some daytime bombing hops at the western
end of the DMZ; it's fairly close by, so we have some gas left
after the bomb runs, so Randy and I have been doing some
sightseeing. The ruins of the French rubber plantations
are in the mountains and on the inland plateaus. We fly
fast and low, in the tops of the thick jungle canopy, hoping
some Gook is not out practicing with his gun. The ruins
are French-style villas and their storage buildings and

workshops. When we spot one of them, we slow down and cruise over it. The buildings are bombed or burned, but the miles of straight rows of rubber trees are still there, covered by the fast-growing jungle.

Things are starting to get kinda weird around here. We had a new pilot check in last week, named Horner. We noticed he was fidgety, but we figured if he got this far he, like the rest of us, knew what he was doing. He went through the local course rules and procedures training and got all his survival gear and was ready to go flying. The night before his first hop, we had a rocket attack, a typical three o'clock twenty-rocket burst with some direct hits in our compound and the sirens going off. Then we heard some gunshots right there in the officers' living area. So we put on our flak jackets and got our pistols out, because we usually didn't hear gunshots right there. Turns out Horner had been sleeping in his guns and combat gear, and when the rockets started, he flipped out and ran out of his hooch shooting into the air and screaming like a crazy man. He calmed down but still had this wild look in his eyes. All us lieutenants pulled the CO aside and told him nobody's flying with Horner, so it looks like Horner goes to wing headquarters where he will file documents for ninety days and then be sent home. I don't think he was ready for combat.

By now, you are probably a big star after your Doolittle gig. In our skit yesterday, we convinced the colonel to play a French whore. It was great stuff. Thanks for the letter.

Semper Fi,
Jay

August 16, 1968

Dear Poet the Pilot,

Your poem touched me. Keep writing. When I fantasize about you, it has always been in some glamorous setting with you as the hero and me as the heroine. I forget to consider the simple luxuries, the sheer importance of loving, having kids, being with someone through thick and thin, making a life out of farming and living each day. I'm not sure it's where my heart lies. I grew up that way, and right now it's not enough. I have this wanderlust that courses through me and tells me about a great big world out there just waiting for me to see and feel and taste and live. So much of my last few years on the farm were spent putting off my dreams and looking death square in the face. I'm not sure I could ever settle for a farming life, but I wish I could. I wish I didn't feel I have to always prove myself just to be worthy of being.

The talent show was a blast. Janice lent me her broad-brimmed rain hat. I made giant paper flowers and pasted them on the brim. I wore a white, high-necked, dotted Swiss blouse, very Victorian looking. I used a tablecloth to create a long skirt and wore a wide patent-leather belt to hold it up. I don't know if I sounded like Liza Doolittle, but I surely looked the part. Some of the staff even came up and told me I was good!

Last week, my day off was cold and rainy. I caught a ride into Bar Harbor with the guys who run the gift shops when they went in to get supplies. In the morning, I took the boat tour around Bar Harbor. The hills are dotted with lots of summer homes of the socially elite, along with the ruins from the fires. The boat was covered, so I stayed dry. I got back to Bar

Harbor in time for lunch and grabbed a sandwich at the drug store. Folks always feel sorry for someone who eats alone, but I enjoyed the solitude. After lunch I walked around the town square. It has a small bandstand and soft green grass for concerts. It had stopped raining by then. I bought Mother a pendant watch and mailed it to her for her birthday.

The local theater was having a Humphrey Bogart festival. They had three movies for the price of one, and I happened by just as the first was starting. I saw _The Maltese Falcon_, _Casablanca_, and _African Queen_. Bogie was great, a little like I have imagined you, with parts of you in each of the movies. In _The Maltese Falcon_, he plays Sam Spade, this killer macho detective (that's the super macho marine). He had two lines that I thought were great. When he was being questioned by the police after the murder of his partner, he said, "Sorry I got up on my hind legs, boss, but you trying to rope me makes me nervous." Use that in your next skit. The second line I loved was when he was going to turn in the femme fatale for murder. He said, "If they send you up for life, you'll get out in twenty years. I'll be waiting for you. If they hang you, I'll never get over you." How cool is that? Of course the other part of you is Rick in _Casablanca_. He's so in love with Ilsa (Ingrid Bergman), and she with him, but in order to protect her, he sends her off with Victor Laszlo, her husband. Now that is true love, to risk your life to save the woman you love. By the way, he doesn't say, "Play it again, Sam." Bogart and Bergman are such great actors. You could see the emotion in their eyes. They captured me and drew me into Rick's American Café. I was there, at least for a few hours.

In _African Queen_, he plays a drunk with a heart

of gold. (You're always talking about getting drunk, but you seem to really care about things.) Katharine Hepburn is a spinster living out in the bush with her missionary brother. When her brother dies, Hepburn (Rosie) inspires Bogie (Charlie Allnut) to believe they can travel down the river, shoot the rapids, and eventually blow up a German gunboat, the Queen Louisa that is controlling the river. She pours out all his whiskey, helps him fix the boat, and he begins to believe in himself. It's hard to think about being as old as they are (at least forty-five) and falling in love. I think I liked this Bogie best of all. They wind up getting married just as they are about to be hung. But at the last minute, the Queen Louisa blows up, and they swim away to safety, singing one of old Charlie's drinking songs. What a great date Humphrey Bogart is!

After the movies, I went to Martino's for dinner. Julie Martino gave me a slice of strawberry pie on the house when I told her you wanted to woo her. She said you would have to kiss her father's ring before you take her out. It's an old Italian custom. A few of the JPH staff came in, and I managed to get a ride back. Thanks for the pie. It was delicious.

This week several of us are going sailing. Only three weeks left before heading back to North Carolina. Got to eat more lobster on the beach before I leave.

"Here's looking at you, kid,"
Ashley

Kathryn Watson on a North Carolina beach.

College student, Kathryn Watson.

View of Jordan Pond and the Bubbles *from the Tea Lawn at the Jordan Pond House, Acadia National Park, Maine.*

*Kathryn Watson serving tea and popovers on the
Tea Lawn at the Jordan Pond House.*

Climbing the Rocks, *a favorite pastime when not working.*

View of the water from the Rocks.

Rockefeller Gardens, Acadia National Park, Maine.

Kathryn Watson playing Liza Doolittle in a talent show.

View of Seal Harbor at Rockefeller's Dock.

View of Sommes Sound from Eagle Cliff.

Sommes Sound.

Motorboat leaving a circular mark in Sommes Sound.

Sailboats in the Sound.

View of Isle au Haut from a boat.

The Ledges *at Echo Lake.*

View of Stonington, Maine, from the ferry.

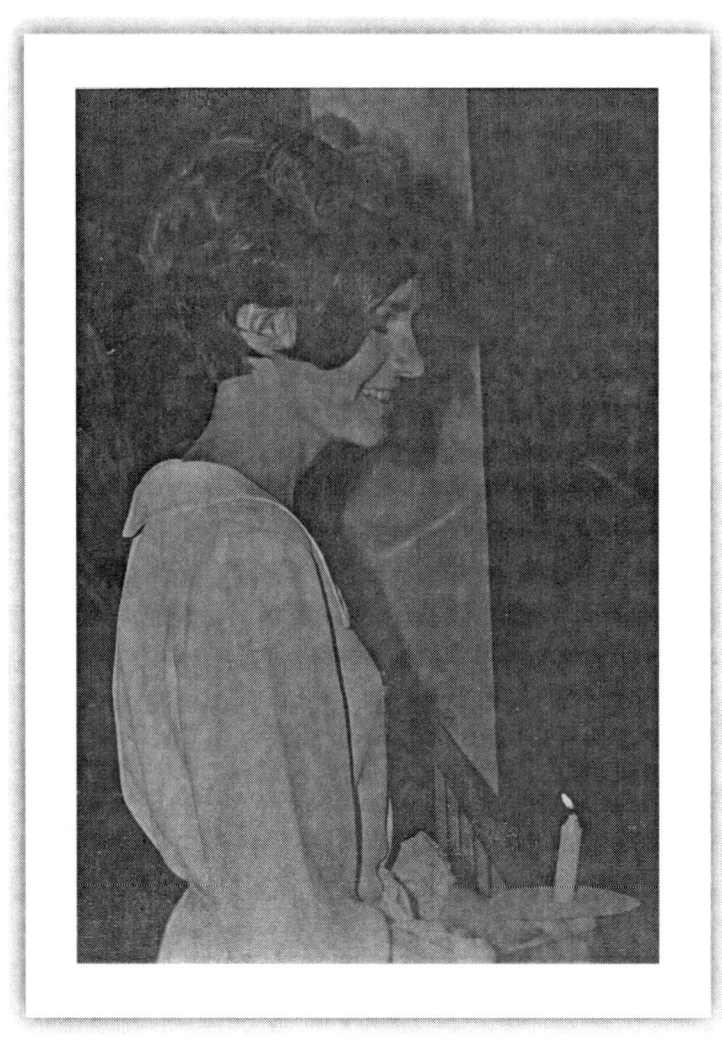

Kathryn Watson at a college ceremony.

21 August '68

Dear Alpha,

> Western Highways
> by Jay Fox

> I set out on the western highways
> To find a place I could do things my way.
> When I got there,
> Things weren't fair,
> Out on the western highways.

> The moon was the same, and each star had a name.
> There were people who made it all blend.
> But the thing that was gone,
> That I'd left back at home,
> Was the thing that leads to an end.

I've managed to make the past two months pass by like they never even existed. I've got 165 missions, and the flying is still good. Between that and my work at the squadron and my daily efforts to stay in shape, I am busy. After nine months in this place, I've run out of things to do trying to kill time, so I just work all day, every day. It ain't bad, really. I still like it here. And it looks like I will go from here to Cherry Point, North Carolina, in about four months. When I get there, I want to find a little house or a trailer that's off by itself and do a little fishing and a little flying and enjoy myself for a while. Of course, I'll be looking for a little farm to buy.

I just got back from two nights in Nakom Phenom on the Thailand–Laos border. The air force runs their combat operations there. We use them for controllers in some of our hops, so we're trying to get a better idea of what is going on from their point of view. There's talk of a new high-tech bombing system, and our group commander picked me to run the combat evaluations, so I'll be flying twice daily for about two weeks checking out this new stuff before anybody else gets to use it. Should be some good flying.

You may call me Captain Jay now. My promotion warrant came in while I was at NKP. I still am not accustomed to the idea of being something besides a lieutenant. I was one for forty months, and I rather enjoyed all of it. Randy is leaving here in a couple of weeks, so it looks like his warrant went to his next station, so for a while here I outrank him. He hates it. It looks like I will fly every day until we quit here, and I should end up with about 225 combat missions. We are short on pilots, so the few of us here are having to earn our wages. Everybody is anxious to leave this place.

When I told you about my trip to Sydney back in May, I did not mention that while I was there I met a girl. Her name is Jennifer Tracey. She is very Australian, older than me, a nurse. I met her on the beach, and she happened to have a few days off, so we went to the mountains on the train. I did not mention her to you because I thought it was something that just happened and was over. Now I've gotten a letter from her. She wants me to come back down. I sure could use a week in Australia, especially after this big weapons evaluation I'm doing. Two colonels and a major are flying here from DC to observe the evaluation, so I'll be meeting with the fat cats after I fly every day, talking about our tests. It'll drive me nuts, so Australia sounds real good, but I don't know if it matters to you. I need some advice here. I've become attached to you and our weekly visits. I trust you. Maybe you can help me figure if I should go back.

You're busting out, and I'm proud of you. My senior

year in high school and the summer after the senior year were so carefree. I had a car and a girlfriend and made some money measuring tobacco for the government. My life was easy, so it makes me smile when you go on in your letters about the really fun stuff at JPH. You had to wait for this chance to stretch out, so enjoy it.

Love,
The Cap'n

August 26, 1968

Dear Captain Kangaroo,

Sooo ... you want to go down to Australia to meet a little filly named Jennifer Tacky. I mean Tracey. Hm ... so you spent several days with her in the mountains. Sooo ... she's older than you. I suspect you "lost all track of time" with Miss Tacky. Hm ... so she's a nurse. Did you play Doctor? First of all, I told you I in no way wanted to limit your freedom or put restrictions on you. Just because I've been saving myself for you shouldn't matter in the least. No, sirree! "Losing all track of time" with just anybody is certainly your business. And Australia is not even a deserted island. There's no way I'm making this decision. You have to make this decision on your own. I have no claim on you, and you have to live with your decisions. I have made a decision to wait for the right person, at least for now. The right person could be you, or it could be someone I don't know yet. Who knows? When you went down to Australia in May, we were just beginning to get to know each other. You had every right to interact with anyone you wanted. Now the difference is we know each other pretty well, better than anyone I've dated because I've shared things with you that were pretty intimate, things I've never shared before in conversation. I will never question what you choose to do, even if you decide to "lose all track of time" with ten Jennifer Tackies. You have to decide what you want and what you can live with. I've certainly done my share of dating this summer. I've had a great time and a great summer. I haven't gone off and spent the night with anyone, except that night on Cadillac Mountain, and it doesn't count because there was a crowd of us and s'mores and no sunrise. Do what your heart tells you to do. Just don't tell me about it unless it was innocent. I really don't want to know. I care about you a lot. I want very much to meet you and enjoy a healthy, wholesome relationship so we can see if all this sharing we've done by mail means anything when we are face-to-face. I really like some of the people here, but I have no clue as to whether they will be long-term relationships. Every day has been a new adventure in freedom and making decisions and seeing new places and discovering who I really am. It's been the greatest summer of my life, and you have been a part of that summer. When you meet me, I may not be the person you've made me into through my letters. I think we will know pretty quickly after we meet. My advice is to follow your heart. You will know the answer and only you. I love you, Jay Fox. But I really love a poet who flies planes and shares his heart and fears and hopes. That Jay Fox is in Vietnam. The same Jay Fox may not need me when he gets to Cherry Point. I may not need him either. I do know I shall never ever forget him, and he will always be in my heart.

Did you hear about Czechoslovakia? I happened to walk through the TV room when a special bulletin came on the news. There were pictures of tanks crushing people who were protesting the lack of freedom. The Soviets mean business. I feel for the people, but I do hope we don't get involved. It's all we need, to be fighting wars on two fronts. I can't believe I just said that. My heart wants those people to have freedom, but I just want you to come home. You don't need to fight another war. You've done your duty.

Mark left today for North Carolina to start a

teaching job. Last night he took me out to dinner and dancing at one of the big old hotels in Bar Harbor. There was a Big Band playing, and we had a great time. We dressed up and enjoyed a special evening. He's one of those people I really like a lot, but I don't think there's any future. When we got back to the JPH, one of the girls met us and said Collins had been crying and crying about Mark leaving. We had planned to smooch a while, but I suggested Mark spend a little time with Collins. I know I'll see him on a football weekend, but Collins is just desperate. It may sound crazy to you, but it just seemed like the right thing to do. See, I'm not dependent on Mark or anyone. It's great to go out and have a good time with him, but he doesn't complete me. I'm not sure any man can. I hope I complete myself. Who knows?

Tomorrow, several of us are going sailing. Two guys from England joined the staff several weeks ago. A few folks like Mark have to leave early, so the Brits are picking up the slack. One of the English guys, Hugh, teaches sailing to the Northeast Rich Kids (NERKs). He is allowed to take out a sailboat whenever he wants, so we are tagging along. I have never been sailing before, so this will be another marvelous adventure. I'll tell you all about it in my next letter. Tomorrow and a week from tomorrow will be my last two days off. I head back to North Carolina in about two weeks. You can write to me one more time here, and I should get it. After that I will be back at school with the same address as last spring.

Congratulations on being made captain. I'm proud of you. Do you think you will make a career of the service? There's something kind of exciting about living all over the world. Making captain at twenty-three is quite an accomplishment. You just might be a general by the time you drive my bus on the campaign trail!

> Remember, I love you!
> Ashley

PS: Forgive my "tackiness" with NERKs. They come to tea in groups of twenty or more and try to see how confusing they can make their orders and then don't tip. Some of the waitresses call them NERPs (Northeast Rich Pigs). Notice that I called them NERKs.

31 August '68

Dear Alpha,

I mentioned in an earlier letter I am an Old Testament freak. I came by it honest. My daddy preached it every Sunday, twice, and on Wednesday nights, and I was always right there, listening whether I wanted to or not. The people in the Old Testament stories worked hard and had little. They were always afraid and troubled but celebrated often. Things never turned out too good for some of them, and they were always looking for a better way, and they all seemed to be worried about what would happen to them when they died. The one thing that drove them was guilt, and guilt was something God did, always threatening to punish his people if they didn't do right. So it was my Old Testament guilt that made me tell Sergeant Barwick to cancel my orders for R&R to Australia. Each person here gets one R&R, but the only way to get a second R&R is to bribe somebody. A man in my hydraulics shop told me his friend, Sergeant Barwick, was in charge of cutting orders for people to go on R&R. So I went to see Sergeant Barwick and asked him what he needed that he couldn't find around here. He's a short, stocky dark-skinned fellow, about twenty-five, maybe part Indian. I know he's from Arizona. He said he needed a bottle of Chivas Regal. The group commander called my squadron one day last week looking for someone to fly a bird to Okinawa to pick up a part, and I volunteered to go. I had heard they had Chivas Regal there. I flew to Okinawa and picked up the part and a bottle of Chivas Regal. This morning I gave the bottle to Sergeant Barwick and told him to keep it for his trouble but to cancel my orders for R&R. You are so cute. And you make me very curious. I am interested in this healthy, wholesome relationship idea you mentioned. I canceled because I would feel guilty going down under knowing that you're the only person I ever wrote poems to. I've chosen to wait three or four months and lose all track of time with you. Plus, Randy is leaving soon, so I want to fly with him every day this and next week before he takes off back to the real world.

I've been dreaming lately. I sleep from breakfast until midafternoon. The sounds of war are everywhere, so the sleep is usually real light, tossing and turning and being semiconscious. But I started dreaming several weeks ago and sleeping so deep I don't wake up even when whole squadrons of fighters are taking off and helicopters are coming and going. I don't put much stock in what dreams mean because I think it's a happenstance sort of thing, but I've been impressed by the relentless recurrence of the same scenes—farm scenes and things that happen on a farm in slow motion that are so trivial, like filling up a water bucket at an outside spigot, and it takes forever. The water is running, but the bucket doesn't get full. And the animals—pigs, cows, horses, mules—are braying and mooing and oinking, anxious to drink the water from the bucket, but the bucket won't fill up. And sometimes the whole dream is just this little farmhouse. There's no movement or people or sound. Just a cute little house, and I keep waiting for something to happen, and nothing happens. Sometimes there is a girl. I don't know if it is you because I've never seen you, the way you move and how you hold yourself, but there is a girl. She stands in the door looking out all the time. The wind blows her hair. Her dress is tight in the wind. She is very womanly. Sometimes she glances at me then back at the horizon. She has a scarf on her head, so I can't see her profile, only her face when she glances. I don't try to understand what it means, but it makes for peaceful sleep.

Fondly took another hit last night. We were pulling off a target, and a fifty-seven-millimeter round went through the right wing. Nobody knows why it didn't go off and blow the whole plane, but it just punched a hole and kept going. Fondly was great. He lost some hydraulics and started losing fuel, but there was no fire, and I was able to keep us level, even when we dirtied up for the landing. Just before we touched down, fire trucks and crash crews everywhere, I asked Randy what he thought. He said, "Let's park on the runway and walk to the bar." That's what we did. Of course, we bought the whiskey. It wasn't as scary this time. About ten miles out when I dirtied up, dropped the gear and flaps, I thought there was no reason why the airplane should be flying. The hole in the wing looked big from my seat. Then I looked at Randy sitting there putting his stuff away and calmly getting ready to land, and I looked at the lights of Da Nang at the far end of the harbor, and I realized there was no way that airplane was going to crash. They dragged it into the hangar this morning. It's a big hole.

You will be back in school, and I will be flying Fondly into Cherry Point sometime in the late fall. We will arrange to meet. I want to get some good North Carolina seafood, and I want to go to some bucolic setting, and I want you to explain to me how you could make me feel like we are together before we ever met.

Love,
Jay

PS: I don't know about the Czechoslovakia thing. Of course, a few years ago nobody had heard of Vietnam. My CO says if I stay in the Marine Corps for thirty years, I will get to fight on every continent except Antarctica, and there's a long shot we might have to go there.

September 6, 1968

Dear Bucolic Buffalo,

Knock me over with a feather, will you? The bets were on here (at least twenty-to-one) that you were R&R-ing in Australia. Was it guilt or love? I've never much believed people stopped anything because of guilt. I think our prisons would be a lot less full if that was the case. What's your theory on that, Mr. Philosopher?

I think I told you I was going sailing. Just call me Admiral Ashley. What a great day we had! Charles Patrick, Rita, Jenny, Hugh, and Harry all piled into CP's '65 Mustang and headed over to the Northeast Harbor Yacht Club. Hugh checked out a great twenty-five footer, and before I knew it, we were out in the open sea. It was cool, definitely sweater weather, and windy. The waves were high, so high we could lean back and touch our heads in the water. Hugh put up the spinnaker, and it felt like we were racing. He gave all of us novices a chance at the helm, and we took turns standing at the mast so we could have our pictures taken. The sun was "brilliant," as the British would say. It was Carolina blue sky (yes, even in Maine), navy blue-gray colored ocean, brisk ocean spray, and crisp cool clean air. It's another memory I've stored in my memory banks for safekeeping. We passed several giant sailing yachts and sailboats. Everyone waved and toasted us just like we belonged to the jet set. Wish you could have been with us because <u>you</u> really do belong to the jet set.

I'm sending Fondly a care package. Last night after I got your letter, several of us sneaked out to get souvenirs from Mt. Desert Island. Two speed limit signs are within sight of each other on the road near

Thunder Hole. Well, there were two signs within sight of each other. I'm sending one to Fondly to use to patch the hole in his wing. I just didn't know what to get him that would make him feel better, and it hit me that a speed limit Band-Aid would be just the thing. Now he'll have a new call number twenty-five on his wing. He'll be unique, distinctive, one of a kind. I thought about an oilcan but didn't think it would mean as much as the highway sign (given your poem). Tell him how saddened I was to learn of his troubles and how proud I am he brought you in safe. You know, wounded and all. He's got to get better given our political career and his part in getting us around the country.

Have you thought about the fact that while you are dreaming in the daytime, I'm dreaming in the nighttime here? I guess that means we are sleeping together. Don't tell my mother. She just wouldn't understand. I'm not sure I know what your dreams mean. I went to the library today and looked up some of the codes in several dream interpretation books. (I couldn't find much information about all the animals.) Some books say every person in the dream represents the person dreaming. In that case, the girl looking out is you. Others say houses represent the self. Other books say the person looking out is someone you are close to. Given my experience and the Psychology 101 course I took last semester, I can definitely say the girl looking out may be me because I have so many dreams and plans, and they won't happen inside. You seem more satisfied on the farm. I've been there, and I am definitely looking out right now. I feel so close to you that if anyone can make me look back in, it would be you. I can hardly wait until you come home. I want to see you, look into those incredibly sensitive eyes, and find out if I'm looking out or looking in.

Have you ever had a perfect day? This week I had my last day off before heading home next Friday. CP and I took off for Isle au Haut, an island reachable only by ferry. We took a picnic lunch and hiked the island before planting ourselves on a rock overlooking the island and the sea and spreading our picnic. A few people live there, without cars, but mostly it's undeveloped land, green, pristine, and lovely. We caught the last ferry back to the mainland, drove to Camden, Maine, and played in the amphitheater. Camden is unique. The water comes from under the stores and flows into the harbor. We went into a store and walked to the back, to a balcony over the water. The sound of water running is always restful, but to hear it and to see it coming out from under the buildings at sunset was a picture I shall never forget. Before heading back, we had supper in a local café where we stole a knife to cut the home-baked bread we had bought on Isle au Haut. I've never stolen anything in my life before, and now in the last two days, I've committed a crime twice. I feel guilty but not guilty enough to take back Fondly's Band-Aid or the knife. What's wrong with me? Tell your dad to pray for me. I guess I'm not the Old Testament scholar that you are. I think it's because women were treated as chattel, and Lot was ready to give his daughters to the mob rather than give up the two angels. Not to mention how Eve is always blamed for the downfall of mankind just because she gave Adam an apple. Somehow those concepts don't sit too well with me and what I want for my future.

You remember I told you about Delores who tried to rescue me from the evil ranger? She grew up in India, a missionary kid. She professes to be a Hindu. Isn't it ironic? Her parents went to save the heathen and lost their daughter in the process. I don't think the Old Testament did much for her either.

Jay, I'm so scared for you. I want so much to meet you, to walk on the beach with you in North Carolina, to hold your hand, to play tag with the waves with you, to eat seafood with you, to dance with you until midnight, and to determine if all these feelings I have for you are real or just fantasy. Every night when I close my eyes, you are in my head, in my thoughts, in my prayers. I breathe deeply, and it's as if you are breathing with me. I pretend I am flying with you, and I actually see the lights of the airport and the fires from the bombs. How can we be half a world apart and feel so close? You used to end your letters by telling Annie you loved her. Tell Fondly I love him for taking care of you and for getting hurt but never giving up, so you were safe.

Will you be home by Christmas break? If you come to Larkinton, I'll walk over the farm with you and show you the little waterfall near the pond behind our house where my dog and cat and I saw a water moccasin sunning itself on a rock. Another trestle is about a mile back (not the infamous one Marlene adorned on class night), and we can walk across it if we are daring. One of the streams near the back pasture has fool's gold in it. There's an abandoned well near the ruins of the old farmhouse that a man rented from Mother. He put in a whiskey still and burned the house to the ground when the still blew up. There are outcroppings of rock in the side pasture, and the old walnut tree I used to climb, and the giant birch that my cousin carved our initials on when I was little. There's the natural spring that provides our water for the house, and the pasture fences to climb over and through and under as we move around the farm, the quiet woods with pine needles softening each step, and the hollow tree some people call a widow-maker. I'll show you where we used to fish and pick blackberries and roll down the hillside and yell out for an echo and the tree where my overweight cousin got stuck. It's all there just waiting for me to show you. It's even beautiful in winter, and it is all part of me, part of who I am. Yes, I'm definitely looking out that door, but I'm also looking back in because I find comfort and peace in all those places.

Emily Dickinson once said, "Home is the definition of God." It's my Old Testament. The land and the trees and the water and the pine needles resting in the quiet wood just waiting for my step. It snowed a few winters back, and the pond froze. A Canadian goose found the pond and a few breaks in the ice. I fed him, and he came back the next year. The squirrel I rescued after the hurricane lives in the woods near the stream. He won't let me hold him now because the dog and the cat usually walk with me, but he talks to me whenever I venture near his nest. I know it's him, and I always leave him grapes. That's my farm I dream about. I'd love to show it to you, share it with you. It may not be where I'm supposed to be in the future, but it is where I came from. I think Emily Dickinson was right.

I love you,
Ashley

11 September '68

Dear Alpha,

A lot of people pass through here, and some of the people bring books or have books sent to them, and then they leave the books here when they go back to the world. Books were accumulating in the hooches and at the clubs and at the flight line, so some enterprising young troopers gathered all the books together and catalogued them and call it a library. Since you've got me started on this poetry and song writing thing, I've been reading up on poetry and sayings, and I have been writing limericks:

> I sat on a fence with some chickens
> Named Jim, Bob, and Joe Dickens.
> We lamented the fact
> That the corn crop was slack,
> And by fall we'd
> All have slim pickens.

I'm not sure what all that means, but when I wrote it, it reached me on some level, and it seems to apply to what's going on here. Anyhow, they've got an interesting collection of stuff at the little library, and they're starting to get some cassette tapes of music. I checked out a Merle Haggard tape and learned me some "Momma Tried"—"First thing I remember knowing was a lonesome whistle blowing. And a young'un's dream of growing up to ride."

It don't get no better than that. And I've learned me a little riff on the chorus.

Guilt or love? Sounds like a thesis. Old Testament vs. New Testament? Could one survive without the other? Is love so complicated we have guilt to keep things straight? Would the New Testament have come to us if all those poor people hadn't been so beat up by the Old Testament? I understand your reluctance to buy into the Old Testament stuff because of the way women were treated, but it's the way it was back then. You can either ignore history, or you can learn from it. It's why I like the Old Testament. It's a great lesson in how not to do stuff. Those people had blind faith in a vengeful God. They were so blind and vengeful that even all the love in the New Testament couldn't save them. They're still looking for deliverance. And I don't know if I'm looking for love or not because sometimes I just don't get this love thing. I thought I loved my high school sweetheart. There were strong feelings and urges. But when I knew I would fly jets, I turned her away. She thought we were going to be married. She was devastated when I told her I loved jets more than her. I didn't want her to be devastated. I let her go because I loved her. I wanted good things for her, but it got all messed up. And the idea of love while I'm here at Da Nang is hard to fit into the program. We have what's called the deep knowledge, the knowledge that today is the last day. Every time I go to chow in the evening, after Grit gets the target assignment and tactical updates at the 1600 hours briefing, I pause before I begin my meal and thank God for this, my <u>last supper</u>. It's hard for me to say, "We're going to be in love, and buy a farm, and have babies, and live happily ever after," because I really don't believe I'll live through my trip to the A Shau Valley tonight. They've got some new guns there, and the gunners are very good. But I've got this funny feeling about you, and it makes me want to survive the A Shau. Is that love? Is love wanting to survive so I can see you? I dunno ...

Thanks for the speed limit sign. A courier from the Wing Headquarters Post Office brought the package by the squadron, special delivery. He "Figured it's a special part you need, sir, to keep the war effort going."

He didn't understand why it was sent by a girl from a resort in Maine. I explained to him you are one of our suppliers, a special contract supplier. It just happened that right after the courier brought the sign to the squadron, we had our daily pilots' meeting, and today was my day to give the weekly safety brief. I talked about how we are all getting short here, won't be here much longer, and sometimes near the end of a tour people start getting slack and lazy and start overlooking details. We're in a business where you can't overlook details, so we all need to slow down, pay attention to what we are doing so we will all survive to leave this place in a few weeks. At this point in my safety lecture, I pulled out the twenty-five MPH speed limit sign and held it up in front of all the pilots. "This is the symbol and the reminder we will all fly safe during our last few combat missions here in Vietnam." I had the metal shop erect the sign outside the flight equipment room so all the pilots will see the sign on their way to their airplanes. The sign is now a fixture in our lives. I could probably originate an invoice and have a check sent to you. After all, you are one of our special contract suppliers. I did not tell anyone the sign was stolen and our special contract person is a thief. Do you eventually want to work for Julie Martino's dad? You could run the international black market in stolen signs, open up a whole new market. I'm sure those Mafia boys get tired of the same old prostitution, drugs, and numbers games. You already have a contract here. You, through the Martino Mafia, will supply all the signs we need here to slow down the war and make it safer. It will ultimately bring us victory here in Vietnam, and you, as the sign supplier, will be hailed by my chief as well as by Don Martino, or Martino the Don. The mob will promote you, and you will be put in charge of, say, prostitution and drugs. It is at that point when Fondly and I will join you. Try to get liquor too. Anyhow, thanks for the sign. Fondly sends his regards. He was fixed immediately. We flew combat the next night.

I have enjoyed sleeping with you. It's a nice image you sent. But I feel like I've missed part of the normal sleeping with experience. The part I've missed is the part I would normally be interested in. But this is not normal. Let me get this straight: I plucked a letter off a bulletin board, out of boredom and curiosity, and wrote to a ditzy college kid, and now all I can think about is getting back to the world and seeing you. I haven't seen your smile. I haven't watched you move. But you're with me all the time, even when I'm flying. When I thunder through the valley, down low at night, and all the gunners are working hard to blow me away, I see you at that moment, straight through the earth, sitting under a tree between classes, eating a Popsicle, and glancing up every now and then to see if I'm there yet. So how did it get from the bulletin board to where it is now? And does that mean it will always be an abnormal thing?

You've painted a lovely picture of Maine. Maybe you can take us there. I'm no Kip Dunlop, but I can tell you some stories about moonlit nights that will get your blood pumping. I like seafood, so we can go to every restaurant up there, and we'll do some comparison eating—"This is just like I remember it" or "Their food's gone to hell since I was here." I don't know if you've picked up on it, but I really like good food. Maybe it's a southern thing. Maybe it's a preacher's kid thing. You can take me on a food tour of Maine. Lead me around by my stomach. And I would love to go to your farm. I always heard a man can't buy a farm and make a go of it; you have to inherit or marry a farm. If I like your farm, I might want you to marry me.

We've heard the outcome of the political nominating

conventions and how the world's largest gathering of perverts tried to sabotage the Democrats in Chicago. Hearing about the chaos there makes me want to stay here. Well, almost. I might actually like your farm.

Love,
Jay

September 16, 1968

Dear Job,

The routine of college has begun in earnest. I wrote "Symphony" for a poetry class, although I changed some of it for you. The assignment was to write a conceit. A conceit, in case you have forgotten, is to make a comparison between yourself and something else. The professor said he was a gas station filling up young minds each day to send them out into the world. For the class, my conceit started with "My life is a symphony." Since you keep bringing up the Old Testament and the New Testament, I changed yours to read a little differently. The teacher actually asked me to read it out loud in class. I hope you like it.

Symphony
by ABJ

Lord, make my life a symphony. Let any discord come in the mornings as I ready myself for the day, tuning and ridding each instrument of my body of inharmonious notes. As the day begins to play, I sound the soft melodies of the violin cascading over the deeper strains of the viola and the cello. The bass grounds me just as the brass lifts me to higher plains. The woodwinds keep me on a solid pathway while the percussion excites me to create new opportunities. My heart sings with this symphony, pumping the energy to melodiously take on the challenges before me. I breathe in syncopated rhythm as your spirit courses through the fibers of my being. Each day brings new tunes and new creations leading to a crescendo of harmony. On that final day of performance, I will pass the baton and move to a heavenly orchestra where I become a fine-tuned instrument twinkling in your fiery firmament, an overture to all that is, all that has been, and the grand finale to come.

I had just been to the convocation with the North Carolina Symphony, so the comparison was easy after the hypnotic effect of the real symphony. Can you believe it? I had never heard a live performance of the symphony. Of course I had heard recorded classical music before but never the real deal. Sometimes I think my life has been lived in a vacuum. I can't seem to crowd everything in that I have missed.

Now back to the Old Testament. Let's take old Job. Why would God test someone like he did Job? God on a dare with the devil took away everything from Job just to prove he was a truly righteous man. What about the significance of Job's first family? Were they just pawns in God's little wager? It's extremely hard for me to understand that God. It's much easier for me to have faith in a God who loved me enough to send someone to save me. It gives me value. Looking at the Old Testament as just a cultural picture of a woman's worth has led many a man to discount women today. Sure, I agree history is history, but the negative impact of that history is tremendous; therefore, the New Testament is closer to my way of interpreting the world. (But not Paul, I don't like him much, except when he says there is "no male or female in Christ.")

My trip home was uneventful. CP took me to the airport. We had talked about driving back together, but I wanted a weekend at home before school, and I wasn't sure about a night on the road with him. My brother-in-law picked me up at the airport. It was great to be home again, but I felt a bit like a stranger. My little nephew was with us on Saturday. We looked outside, and a doe was in the yard with twin babies. Johnny is almost four, and he was fascinated by his close look at nature. We followed Mama Doe from room to room and window to window. She communicated with her little ones with tail movements. I was trying to explain to Johnny how unusual it was to see twins. He responded with a matter-of-fact explanation. "It might be like Mommy and Gerald's mommy. She keeps me sometimes, and Mommy keeps Gerald sometimes." Now that I think about it, I'm not sure if the deer was babysitting or if she had twins.

Let's talk about love. I don't exactly see love as something you give up to go fly jets. I know you say you did this for her (your high school sweetheart), but something just doesn't ring true. I mean when you love somebody, you go through whatever it takes to make life work. You stick together through the good times and the bad. You're faithful and true and dedicated to that one person. It's what I want. Someone who loves me more than anyone else, someone who thinks I'm prime, choice. A person who sees me as being better than I really am, so I can live up to that expectation and actually be better than I am. Of course I want someone who thinks I'm beautiful and has the hots for me too, but also someone who is tender and gentle and really concerned about how I feel. I want to be ecstatic about him, steadfast, true blue, but I can only be that if I am sure he values me for who I am, even our differences. I don't want much, do I? Any takers?

You must never write about the black market and stolen signs again. Don Martino has people in the mailrooms all over the country scanning letters. When you least expect it, you may wake up with a Mule Crossing sign in your bed or there may be sugar in Fondly's gas tank. Why, I've heard tales about lobsters in a man's underwear and fireworks going off just when you're stealing a Yield sign. It's not pretty, like Julie Martino. Keep your head about you, Captain, and you may live to see Cherry Point. Drop your guard again like you did in your last letter, and I may have to turn you in. I'm pretty high up in the organization, and I will do nothing to risk my status. If a man kisses you on the forehead, even in your skits at the Officers' Club ... well, I wouldn't go out flying that day. You're being watched.

Your high degree of interest in food and eating is an obvious example of the old adage "The way to a man's heart is through his stomach." I fear that if you continue to see me eating too many Popsicles underneath that tree, I shall be of Olympic proportion when we finally meet. I do understand that your fascination with food is a southern custom carried down for generations by good country folks. I remember going to my grandmother's as a small child. My great-aunt Daisy and her husband, Uncle Willie, lived at my grandmother's and took care of her. My grandmother had rheumatoid arthritis and was wheelchair bound. She died when I was five. Aunt Daisy would prepare sumptuous Sunday dinners, and there would be two or three tables of people for meals. She would have fried chicken, mashed potatoes, peas, butterbeans, snaps, stewed tomatoes, baked sweet potatoes, biscuits, ham, corn pudding, fried okra, turnip salad, candied sweet potatoes, corn bread, banana pudding, lemon pie, chocolate cake, and bread pudding. There was always ice tea and coffee.

Aunt Daisy used to sneak me Postum at breakfast, and I would pretend I was drinking coffee. She would pretend like we were fooling Mother. I felt so grown up. Aunt Dora, another of my grandmother's sisters, was seated at the table one day when she said, without cracking a smile, "I wish I was a mule." Everyone turned to Aunt Dora, and she continued, "If I was a mule, I would kick all the lemon out of this pie."

Now that I've listed all those southern delicacies, do you love me?

I love you,
Ashley

21 September '68

Dear Alpha,

> The brass at the top controls me.
> A ditzy coed unfolds me.
> I must be going,
> Like old Georgie Cohen,
> Home for the crowds to behold me.

I know I've mentioned this before, but it looks like we'll be going home soon. Did I tell you the same thing in the spring and again in the summer? It looks kinda real this time. Randy left yesterday. He decided to rotate early instead of sticking around and flying home with the rest of us. He is going to flight school and is anxious to get started. He wanted to be a pilot when he was commissioned, but the pipeline into flight school was full then, so he went to navigator school just so he could get into airplanes and fly in the war. When he left here yesterday, there were two hundred enlisted men who believed he is the greatest officer in the Marine Corps. He contributed more to the squadron in his year here than anyone else ever has. And we got our two hundred missions together. Grit is the first crew ever to get two hundred. I don't know who to fly with now. The other navigators are my friends, and I've known them for a while, but it just won't be the same to climb into Fondly with anybody else but Randy. We never had to talk about what we were going to do. We were a crew, the three of us, out there doing our job. I'll let you know about our rotation when things are more certain, but it looks like I'll be home by December. Everybody is anxious to get away from here and get back to the world. Last week I ordered a 1969 GTO from the factory. It will be at a dealership in Raleigh when I get back. It's British Racing Green with a BRG convertible top, a 389-cubic-inch engine with solid lifters, a four BBL, four-speed Hurst, AM/FM, A/C, power windows, and a tan leather interior. Thought I might need a little something to ride around in out there on my new farm.

Remember when I told you if you know where you're headed, and you work hard every day, you have earned my respect, even if you are a girl? It's still true. It would have pissed me off if they'd told me I couldn't fly jets because I'm a boy. You repeat the "held back because I'm a girl" theme often. I don't know if it's because you have actually been held back, or you're afraid you will be held back if you try something big that is traditionally done by men. You quote Bible references to the man-woman thing, so it must be on your mind. I use our letters to sound off about how scared I am when I get back from a bad hop. I can't just walk into the Ready Room after a hop, with all the other pilots sitting around drinking coffee, and announce, "Man, am I scared shitless!" So I put it in the letters. Use me, darling. Figure out all the Old Testament vs. New Testament and woman's worth stuff. I think you'll spend your life doing something great, so go ahead and figure out the girl thing so it won't be in your way.

I've edited this a bit, but I loved your love discussion in your last letter, so I pulled out the essence of your words:

Ashley's Love Litany

Whatever it takes, stick together,
Faithful, true, and dedicated.
Love me more than anyone;
Think I'm prime, choice.
See me as better than I really am.

Think I'm beautiful,
Hots for me too.
Tender, gentle, concerned,
Ecstatic, steadfast, true blue.

Aunt Lula was my granddaddy's sister. They were raised down in Nash County on a tobacco farm. Everybody around there farmed, and farm people didn't get to town much, especially the girls. Girls were expected to marry young and run the house and help with the farm. Lula married the boy whose farm joined theirs. Lula was not like most of the other girls. She was very bright, but mostly she had a muse. Her art took the shape of a formal garden. Out there behind her farm house, down in Nash County, was a formal, European-style garden with its carefully drawn paths and evergreen screens and perennial borders and annual beds and statues. The people around her thought she was crazy. Her husband was crude and uneducated, though he did raise a good tobacco crop. He thought she was wasting her time messing with her stupid garden. When it came time to do big, important stuff in the garden, Lula would throw a fit. She would get down on the ground and writhe and froth at the mouth and scream a fit. They would send her off to the mental ward at Dix Hill in Raleigh. She would stay for a few days then come home, frail, and her case worker would recommend she recuperate for a couple of weeks, maybe spend a little time with a hobby. So for two weeks Lula could do the bed work and make permanent improvements that had to be done in that season to keep her garden working. No one bothered her during that time. She was recuperating. She never had any children. I can remember going there when I was real little and seeing that garden, surrounded by the mule barn and the pack house and the corn crib and the hog pen and all that goes on at a tobacco farm. I didn't understand why the garden was there. I asked Daddy one time why the garden was there. He said it was something Lula did. He said Lula wasn't right. But just before I came over here to Da Nang, we went to a family reunion, and Lula was there. She was almost ninety-five years old and an invalid. When she got to the reunion, they needed somebody to lift her out of the car and onto a chair in the building. They must have thought I looked strong because they asked me to lift her into the building. I went to the car and got my arms under her small frame and lifted her out of the passenger seat. She started hollering, "Who are you? Where are we going?" hollering loud. Somebody said, "Lula, this is Alford's boy's boy." She was still hollering. Everybody at the reunion seemed to expect it of her. Her face was right in front of mine as I carried her, and I looked into her eyes while she was looking at me, and there was somebody at home in there. Lula wasn't crazy. She was just trapped by circumstances.

So, my darling, don't end up like Lula. And I guess your first big step is to not marry some ignorant slob who farms. Meet me first. Decide later.

Love,
Jay

September 26, 1968

Dear "Oh My Darling,"

You sweet thing! You want me to use you. Now most girls I know don't want to feel used, but you, you tell me to use you. It's the whole difference between guys and girls. Girls feel cheap when they're used, and guys want to be used and used and used. How do men and women ever get together when their whole orientation toward the world is completely opposite? I guess you can call it Ashley's Theory of Use. I do thank you for your willingness to let me sound off about the tribulations of women. You said yourself that you would hate it if you couldn't fly planes in the war. I might be able to get a pilot's license, but I could never fly two hundred combat missions, because women cannot be in combat. You're always talking about having kids. Suppose you had a daughter that you loved better than life itself. Whatever she wanted to be, you would support. But society will not let her be anything but girl things. I suspect you would be sad for her because you know how important it was for you to decide to fly jets, and just because she is a girl, she can't make a decision like you did. Do you think my parents wanted a girl when I was born?

Tell me one thing. Did Aunt Lula have the dreaded little toe disease? I like the idea of having fits and frothing at the mouth to get my way. Her destiny as a woman was pretty limited, but she beat the system. You come from pretty strong stock. Can you holler too? What a great way to get people off your case. I think I'll try an Aunt Lula fit on the last day of class. What a cool exit! I like Aunt Lula.

Think long and hard about this farming idea. I can tell you from experience it is not an easy life. In the late summer when we used to harvest tobacco, the days were long and tiring. We got up about four thirty. I always handed tobacco. In the early mornings, the tobacco leaves were cold and wet. My hands and arms would be covered with tobacco gum by midmorning. Mama would hand tobacco all morning and then go fix lunch (dinner, as we called it) for all the hands. We all came back after dinner and handed tobacco most of the afternoon. The last job of the day was hanging the sticks of strung tobacco on the tiers in the barn. Daddy would sleep on a cot by the barn and keep a fire going in the flues until the tobacco was cured. No matter how hard I scrubbed my hands and fingernails, I could taste tobacco gum whenever I put a biscuit to my mouth or handled food. The best part of the day was midmorning when Daddy would go buy Pepsis or Cokes and giant sugar cookies. You have never tasted a delicacy like sugar cookies with a hint of tobacco gum. We all got to take a break then. By the time my hands were back to normal the next week, we would be harvesting the next leaves that had ripened on the stalk. Once in a while, Daddy would let me ride the mule when he brought the last slide of tobacco to the barn. I am sure I was a sight to behold. Tobacco gum all over my hands and arms, and mule hair and mule sweat on my legs!

After the curing, we had to tie the tobacco so Daddy could take it to market. Uncle Euclid helped us tie it, and that's when he told me the story about being baptized. He was pretty old and had served in World War I. He told me about being a serviceman on a bus and sitting beside a woman with a crying baby. The woman was trying to get the baby to nurse. The baby kept crying and not nursing, and the woman in her frustration threatened the baby with, "If you don't nurse, I'm going to give it to that man over there."

Mother and Daddy used to plant huge gardens. Guess who had to chop, weed, pick tomatoes, pick beans, shell peas, and then help can it all? Mama's hands were made of steel, and she would pour boiling water over the tomatoes so the peeling would come off easier. We had to pick up those tomatoes and peel them. My poor hands will never be on fingernail polish commercials! Daddy planted corn and running peas so the vines would wind around the corn stalks. Guess who had to chop the weeds? I'm talking about acres and acres because the corn was used to feed not only us but the livestock too.

Equipment was always breaking down, and we never had much money. (Oops, I forgot to mention chopping and picking cotton.) Mama did let me take my lunch to school—I never want to see a bologna sandwich again in my life—and I saved my lunch money in a Christmas savings plan at the bank to buy Christmas presents. I think I got fifty cents allowance a week, but I was never paid for work on the farm or for cutting the grass or cleaning out Mama's flowers.

Think about it. It's not all fun. Why don't you spend the next twenty years getting to be a general, taking me all over the world with you, and then retire to that farm? You can buy it now. When you retire, you'll have a nice retirement income, and you will still be young enough to do the work. That way you won't be dependent on a bad crop or too much rain or too little rain. If everything breaks down and the crops fail, you won't lose the farm, and you'll have enough money to live on. You can fly planes, and I can have a baby or two and write about all those exotic places we live. After you buy the farm, we can build a little log cabin retreat when you have time off. I could bring the children to the country in the summer, and you could fly in and join us as much as possible. When you retire, we could make the house a little more comfortable, and I could write, and you could burn leaves and grow corn and raise cattle. We could replicate Aunt Lula's garden as a tribute to her, maybe even get someone to make a little statue of her lying on the ground frothing at the mouth. The children would bring their children, and every night we would sit on the porch swing and look at star-spangled skies and talk about all the places we had seen together and how smart the grandchildren are and how proud we are of our family and how we danced in the street in Paris and how we swam in the Mediterranean and how we took the children to the zoo when we lived in San Diego, and remember the first time the baby went to the beach and saw the ocean. And we could talk about how nice it is and was to have the farm to always come back to and especially now to have this quiet time together in our sunset years on our little farm. And I could help you do things because you know I'm capable even though I'm a girl. I'll be a famous author or maybe secretary of state, and we can go on book tours, but always we come back to the farm. (Please do not raise tobacco. Cotton is okay, but I can taste that tobacco gum now.) Fondly could marry a John Deere and live with us too. He could have little riding lawn mowers and gliders and whatever kind of family he wanted. And we could put the speed limit sign on the path leading down to the house to remind us all to slow down and savor life. That's what it's all about, savoring each day, looking forward to new adventures, living each moment, and remembering.

Gee, I can't wait to meet you. Are you a good kisser? I'm great at it. In fact, I'm imagining our first kiss right now.

I love you,
Ashley

1 October '68

Dear Alpha,

Okay ... let's see ... all I've got to do is survive this,
kiss you, and keep flying jets; then we make babies and
go around the world and settle down on the farm and play
with the grandkids. I'd rather buy an old run-down place
or a place with no buildings, just dirt and plants, trees
and some cleared bottomland. I want to build the farm.
I want to make it like I want it. Not tobacco and cotton.
They take too much from the soil. They are too complex
and expensive. There's a catch phrase in the Marine Corps:
Keep It Simple, Stupid—or KISS. I want to keep it simple on
my farm. The buildings, the infrastructure, fences, roads,
food crops, cattle. I want to do the work, dig the ditches
for the plumbing pipes, cut the trees for the lumber in the
buildings, start with a small herd and breed the cattle I
want, start a long-range tree program for the grandkids.
Our children will love it there, growing up learning how
to do honest work. And you can conquer the universe from
our farm. Women will be powerful by the time we get going
good, and you will have it all: living close to the land,
gorgeous kids, a brilliant social agenda, married to a
war hero. And I'll stay on the farm and work and build the
place. You can travel all you want. After this vacation
I'm on now, I don't think I'll do much getting around for a
while. You will be paid for what you do, and you can give
me some money for beer.

The past week has been a good one. The squadron has
cut down on its flying, so I'm getting one combat hop every
two days. I have to do a comprehensive flight evaluation on
each of the twelve airplanes before the squadron takes
off across the ocean, so I won't have much time off between
now and the time we leave here. I try to schedule my time
off at midday so I can devote a couple of hours each day

to a body beautification program—acquiring a suntan and staying in shape. Right now I have the best suntan of my entire life, and the conditioning is coming along fine. I can maintain my tanning program en route. I figure I have done my share here, with 213 missions (more than anybody has ever flown in this squadron as a pilot), and fifteen air medals and one Distinguished Flying Cross approved so far. So I am investing most of my energy in testing the airplanes in preparation for the TRANSPAC (flying across the Pacific). The monsoon will start soon, just like it was when I got here a year ago, so we are leaving at the right time. The weather should be good after we get away from the mainland. I shipped a large box of uniforms and various items yesterday, including all the stuff on my Blowed Away List. It will all sit at Cherry Point until I get there. Everybody is anxious to leave this place. It won't be long now.

This love thing is a real struggle for me. I broke up with the girl at college because I didn't want to be affected by love stuff while I'm flying in combat. I still do not want to be affected by love. I think the near miss the night I forgot to turn my lights on was probably because I was thinking about you. You're so charming and fun. All those plans of yours are beautiful. But I'm still flying. What I can imagine is coming home to meet you, and we immediately set the plan in motion—your plan, my plan, doesn't matter—and the plan works, and our lives are good, and we live happily ever after. But I can't think about kissing you or touching you, or you touching me, or the two of us truly becoming one because I'm still flying. I don't want to become someone else's loss. It would be a loss for my family if I got blowed away during my last few nights here. Why expand the grief to you? Why let it affect your life? Our eyes have never met. I've never watched you move. So, love? The only way I can do this is if we set a rendezvous and just strike up whatever the movement and the eye contact produce. Conquer the universe together? Yes. Have a big ol' time? Yes. Maybe we fall in love in time, okay? Help me out here. Be Old Testament. Be Alpha female. Intellectually, I know the Gooners know better than to mess with the two-hundred-mission Grit. But Randy is not here, and I don't want you to count on me until I'm there.

Semper Fi,
Jay

October 15, 1968

Dear KIS, Stupid,

My daddy always taught me to take responsibility for my actions. He said blaming someone else for my mistakes was wrong. I don't blame you when I don't complete a paper on time. Don't blame me for the lights on the plane. I have loved writing to you and fantasizing and dreaming about what it might be like to meet you and love you and play with you and sing country songs with you. I have also continued to date here and in Maine. Next weekend I'm going to Tennessee to see CP for his homecoming weekend at the University of the South. I really like him. I don't plan to sleep with him, but I do plan to enjoy being with him. Especially since you are so afraid of being close to me. I know your intentions are positive, but get real. You've been just as much a part of this fantasy as I have. Just suppose instead of causing your problem with the lights, I've been a part of keeping you alive because you have someone to come back to instead of nothing and no one. And furthermore, I've never known a farm woman with a "brilliant social agenda, gorgeous kids, and a war hero husband" who conquered the universe. When I get married, I don't want to be gone every night, and my focus when I have children just might be the children. It's why I've got to feel like my life has been worthwhile before I settle into that kind of routine. Besides, I've got two and a half years of college left, and more if I go to graduate school. Do you really want someone you can make a life with who has real hopes and dreams of her own, or do you want someone to just hang out with or someone you don't have to be serious about but who meets all your physical needs? Well, Captain Marvel, I'm not just some blip on your radar screen. I'm real and soft and kind and loving and eager and excited about life. If you want an interesting life, I'm someone you'll never get bored with. I'll always be dreaming of the next adventure, the next opportunity, and the possibilities that exist. I've had enough of being second best. You can't just pull me toward you and then push me away. I don't know if we'll like each other face-to-face. You may turn out to be a three-hundred-pound gorilla for all I know, but I have loved writing to you, and I would like to get to know you. "Here's looking at you, kid!" (Do you think the loss would be any easier for me if something happened to you now? Suppose I were to get killed on my flight to Chattanooga next week. Would you not feel the grief or loss?)

Annie says you are just a typical jock marine. She says that if you had any sense, you would never be in Vietnam. She's getting heavily involved in the antiwar movement. She was in Chicago for the Democratic convention, and she has been traveling to Chapel Hill for SDS (Students for a Democratic Society) meetings. She tells me very little about the meetings, begs Jena and me to attend, and she almost got arrested last week. The three of us are rooming together in a suite of rooms on a freshman hall. We serve as resident advisors with no pay, just a nicer living space and the chance for all three of us to live together. Jena stays out of politics. She has started playing tennis and will probably make the tennis team. Last year she played her first game of tennis with me and then took a tennis course. She's a great athlete.

While I'm in Tennessee, I'll check on a country

music recording contract. Maybe you'll fall in love with a guitar-shaped pool if you can't fall in love with me.

Fondly,
Ashley

20 October '68

Dear Ashley,

(I'd had right much whiskey when I wrote that last letter, and I didn't read it after I wrote it, and I mailed it that night but I did keep a copy. I can tell from your reaction it was not well received. I probably did not properly address some of our key issues. So let's give her another shot.)

It looks like you'll have to expect me when you see me, sometime between Thanksgiving and Christmas. I wrote to my parents asking them to stop the <u>Piedmont Progress</u> and the Baptist Church Bulletin. If you mail a letter after the fifth, I probably will not get it, so try to send me one more letter and include your phone number at school. There is no way to tell how long it will take to get across the ocean—depending on weather and airplane breakdowns. Two to three weeks is a good estimate. If you have a map of the Pacific, you can follow the flights: Subic Bay (Philippines), Guam, Wake, Midway, Hawaii, El Toro. I will probably have to spend a few days in California then should be free to fly home. There is still a possibility I will fly a sick bird to the Norfolk rework facility. That requires a test pilot, and I'm the only one around right now. I'll write to you from each island as I progress with the TRANSPAC, then I'll call you when I get to California. I'm including my home address in Piedmont if you need to write to me while I'm en route.

The test hops are almost done. I've finished ten airplanes and lack only pressurization testing on the other two. It involves going to fifty-two thousand feet and doing some maneuvers. From that high up (ten miles), you can see the curve of the earth. Land looks like a map because you can't distinguish towns or man-made structures except the roads and the airports. On each test hop, I spend about twenty minutes doing acrobatics, wringing out the airframe. It is violent stuff pulling 6 Gs and constantly transitioning from vertical to horizontal maneuvering. I'm still flying combat every other night. We're trying to root out some nasty gun positions up north. It ain't pretty. Our sister squadron lost a bird and a crew yesterday. I've got a new navigator. He's good, but he's not Randy.

What I like about you is your charm, the things you tell and the way you tell them. I know I'd never get bored with you because I never know how you'll react, and it's always fun to see what you'll say next. You have this wonderful, pure logic in your arguments that give you authority, a quality I admire. I know your voice is soft, and you are straightforward when you speak. I imagine you move with great confidence and grace. I can see us walking on a beach in winter. No one else around. The spray and the cold breeze and the gulls feeding and squawking. I have warm hands, and yours are cold, so I hold your hand, and we take short steps, and we look at the same things at the same time. The tide is going out. The beach is getting wider. I am grateful to you because you have helped me remain calm during my year here. (I would never blame you for the lights-out near-miss incident. I was probably trying to point out that your presence is always with me. It was a compliment to you that you have penetrated my consciousness in a year of chaos.) You have given me hope, and you have caused me to dream, and I do want to walk on that beach with you. I remember the uncertainty of your first letters. You've grown so much in the last year, and I've done some changing. We've done all that together, so we have a past now. Please enjoy your friends. But save a place for me.

There is one thing you must understand. The Gooks are getting the shit kicked out of them over here. They are losing tens of thousands of their people, but they will not stop now because they know they have stumbled into a generation of worthless Americans, a failed generation. All the Gooks have to do is take their losses, sacrifice their people, until the failed generation of Americans (draft dodgers and protesters) prevails. Annie and her friends give hope to these evil people and cause them to continue in spite of military defeat. The Gook leaders will let all their people die waiting for the sickness in America to win out. And that sickness will prevail because this generation of Americans is so much a failure. That's really why I left college. I looked around and saw the wimps and the twistos and the perverts who will ultimately ruin what could have been a great America. I did not want to be a part of the destruction of a nation that will never recover from this failed generation. Please don't let those people around you suck you into their world. If you go there, you'll always be a failure. You're too good to go there.

It seems strange to talk about going to that world because it seems like I've been here forever. It will be good to relax for a change. I will look for one more letter from you, then I will write to you from the islands.

Love,
Jay

October 28, 1968

Dear Mr. Space Man,

When you are up there, ten miles in the heavens looking at the curve of the earth, I'm down here looking up at wispy clouds in a cool fall blue Carolina sky watching for a silver dot streaking into view. I'm with you up there, you know. I see it all through your eyes like I've never seen it before. I love it when we go horizontal, then vertical, and then spin down only to pull up and move toward the horizon. I don't think I would like learning all the technical jargon, but I would love to be riding with you in the cockpit, seeing the world from outer space. Lindbergh's wife used to fly in the seat behind him in those old planes. She was the one he trusted just like you trust Randy. What a great team they made! When someone kidnapped and later killed their baby, from what I have read, they grew even closer. Isn't it strange how some people overcome adversity and others never get over it? I don't think my parents ever got over the loss of my brother. Daddy withdrew from the family, and Mother consumed herself with me. Daddy used to play with other children, cousins and friends' children, but he never played with me very much. He had lost a twin brother as a young child. I guess he thought if you get too close, something might happen. I miss him this fall more than last year. One year at Thanksgiving he let me walk with him when he went bird hunting. I didn't have a gun, but I loved walking through the woods with him and the bird dog. We didn't talk much, and he walked fast. Sometimes I had to run to catch up. It was a clear, cold November day. The sun was high in the sky (about as high as you are when you test planes) and eye-squinting bright. All the leaves were cushioning the ground, and the evergreens were the only color in a maze of burnt sienna hues. As I think back on it, it was like walking into a sepia (different shades of brown) painting with an occasional splash of green. It smelled fresh and clean, washed in natural pine scent, and the sounds of our feet, the dog running, or the flutter of birds were the only noises. I don't think he got a bird that day, although I do remember Mother cooking quail a few times in my lifetime. It didn't matter to me about the hunt. The best part was being with Daddy, just me by myself. It didn't even matter that we didn't talk.

How did you know I have cold hands? Since you are coming home in the winter, you can be my official hand warmer. I've got mittens, but they never seem to warm my hands enough. I like the idea of walking on the beach in winter. I've never had that experience, although walking in the water in Maine last summer felt like winter. You paint a pretty picture.

My trip to CP's homecoming at Sewanee was party-filled and great fun. Everyone went from one fraternity party to the next. The parties were open to anyone, and CP had friends in every house. It was so different from here, where fraternity parties are pretty much just for that fraternity. We went to each one and then went back to the ones with the best bands before heading to his fraternity house. I stayed at one of his professor's homes who takes in the out-of-town dates on party weekends. The professor's wife fixed buffet breakfasts, and several girls stayed in the spare bedrooms. I got to fly first class on my way home because it was the only seat left on the plane that hadn't been assigned. It was a lovely weekend, but I didn't feel as close to him as I had in Maine.

His school is filled with wealthy and somewhat superficial people. His father is a doctor. His older brother attends the school too, and I sometimes felt I was intruding on a closed club. It's funny how things can change in such a short time.

I beg to differ with your "worthless Americans" assessment. I can understand your reasoning, but I don't happen to think that our country is "going to hell in a handbasket" because people are protesting the war. You yourself have questioned the merits of what you are doing. If human life is of so little value the North Vietnamese are willing to sacrifice thousands of their people, it wouldn't matter what people did to protest the war. Think back to the Second World War. People weren't protesting then. Japan would never have given up if we hadn't dropped the atomic bomb. They valued their people so little they sent their pilots on suicide missions. Individual lives were not important. It took major devastation to end that war. Because of what we have learned about that kind of devastation, we're not willing to do that in Vietnam, so the fight continues and continues and continues. I don't think it is a failed generation. I'm a part of that generation, and so are you. I don't happen to think we are failures, so don't generalize and lump me in with your failed generation. A lot of good people are over in Vietnam fighting, and a lot of good people over here are protesting a war that could go on forever. It's no failure to disagree about issues. We are failures when we fail to respect and honor each other even when we disagree. My fears for Annie are that she is getting into something she hasn't thought out reasonably, and that she will then do something without thinking about the consequences. I love her. She is one of my two best friends. She has made me see the world differently. I don't have to agree with her to appreciate how she has opened my eyes. I just want her to be safe like I want you to be safe.

Come home, Jay. I need you.

Love,
Ashley

October 29, 1968

Dearest Jay,

Uncle Euclid used to tell a story about driving to Norfolk, not too many years ago (before his eyes kept him from getting his license renewed). He accidentally turned onto the wrong road. It was a country road, sparsely populated. After driving for a while and not seeing any recognizable landmarks, he pulled into a little country service station. Uncle Euclid began to ask for directions as the storekeeper began to size up the old man who stood before him, apparently lost. After Uncle Euclid told of his predicament, the storekeeper bluntly asked him, "Are you in your right mind?" Uncle Euclid, never at a loss for words, replied, "I believe I am, but I am lost."

I know you didn't expect to see another letter on the heels of the last, but I must share with you thoughts that keep running through my mind, "my right mind." I am so excited about your homecoming and the opportunity to see you that I hardly sleep at night. I am tense and anxious because I fear I won't live up to your expectations. I'm also afraid my moral high ground will turn you off, and you will immediately dump me for someone who is more ready to meet your physical needs. All my life, my mother and my church have told me to wait to have sex with the man I marry. I'm so attracted to you from your letters I'm afraid I will do something stupid and not be able to live with myself if things don't work out with you. I want to finish college and have a career. If there was ever Old Testament guilt, I'm experiencing it now. You haven't even held me in your arms, and I'm already feeling guilty about what might happen. Writing to you last January started out as my good deed for the day. It turned into something far greater than a good deed. With each letter I have been able to clear out some of the clutter and know myself more deeply. You have given me that gift, for it is like a gift to better understand myself. Because of you, I know what I must do to fulfill my hopes and dreams and desires. I don't know all the particulars, but I do know I have to want it, plan it, and then do it. When you come into the mix, I want you too, but I don't know how to plan for you in the midst of all those big dreams I have. At least not right now. So many women fail to finish college because they think the passion of the moment is the answer. A lot of unhappy women are living in trapped lives. While you are not here, I can think rationally. When you get here, I may be putty in your hands. Jay, how can I want you so badly and still accomplish all those things I've told you about? I know you grew up like me. I know your experiences in Vietnam this year with all of its danger and excitement have caused you to see things differently from your Southern Baptist heritage. My college experiences and last summer in Maine have enhanced my perspectives on a lot of life issues, but the sex issue is still a bit fuzzy. I've made conscious decisions not to let myself get into compromising positions. I still don't drink, and I don't think alcohol will be a huge part of my life. I don't feel as strongly about drinking as I did growing up, but it's not something I need to make it through the day. We are different in several ways, and I'm afraid those differences will doom us, or I will do something that will doom me because I care so much about you. The wrath of my conscience is pretty Old Testament. That's why the New Testament gives me hope.

You probably don't need a letter with all my

insecurities blurted out just as you prepare to leave for home, but I may not be much good at telling you these things when we meet, so I had to tell you now.

If I can know, have some kind of assurance that you will help me work through these things, I won't be so anxious. I'm too much into my head as I wait for you.

ABJ

PS: The phone number on the hall is 772-8659. Classes on MWF are at 9, 10, and 11; TT 9, 11:30, and Lab on W from 2–4. I'm almost always on the hall at 1:00 p.m. and after 8:00 p.m.

Fancy Gal
by Ashley Beth Justice

When I was young, all I wanted was to be married to
    my man.
My heart was free, my mind was strong ... Oh I had
    such plans.
On my weddin' day, my long blonde hair was with
    ribbons tied.
I didn't know what my mama knew, only that she
    cried.

My man, he is a farmer, works from sun to sun.
He said I was his fancy gal, he promised me such fun.
We ran off on a Sunday, got hitched on a winter's day.
Worked the land of a tenant farm, with very little pay.

Now twenty years have passed me by, my hair is
    turnin' gray.
My man who promised me such fun is gone by break
    of day.
I rise and stoke the fire up when he crawls out of
    my bed.
Got chores to do, cows to milk, children to be fed.

I walk outside, feed the chickens, see wood I need to chop.
Come back in, sweep the floor, close the door with
    the stop.
It wasn't always like this, I once had lots of plans.
Now it's cook the breakfast, clean the clothes, wash
    the pots and pans.

The baby, she's a cryin'. There's fever goin' round.
The oldest one, he's out all day, only hunts or goes to
    town.

The girls, they need new dresses, and their shoes are
   mighty worn.
I guess I'll send them out today in feed sacks that are
   torn.

My mama told me early on that a woman's work was
   hard.
I must go pick the beans, hang the wash, and rake
   across the yard.
Got meals to fix, water to draw, lite wood to collect.
Old man hangin' round, wants my daughter, I suspect.

My man, he drinks his whiskey and snores the night
   away.
I get up, sit by the fire, and silently I pray.
Lord, don't let my girls marry a farmer like I did.
Let them get some booklearnin', keep their bodies hid.

The baby whimpers in her crib, I rub her feverish
   head.
Stoke the fire one more time then climb into my bed.
He feels me near, wakes and holds me, then goes back
   to sleep.
Another baby on the way, my belly moves, my eyes
   begin to weep.

It wasn't always like this, I was his fancy gal.
He used to bring me hard candy and call me pretty Sal.
The baby starts to cry again, I rock her by the fire.
He stirs and gets up early, must go fix fence wire.

Another day has started, I pat water on my face.
I stretch and yawn and dress, sit down and say grace.
The children are excited, school is startin' soon.
The harvest, almost in, we planted by the moon.

To Any Soldier

The day has gone by quickly, this day is almost done.
Supper finished, dishes washed, my hair up in a bun.
I go out on the porch to sit a spell, reflect on what's
    to come.
The winds are cool, my body shivers, my hands are
    almost numb.

My man, he is a farmer, he works from sun to sun.
When I was young, he courted me and promised so
    much fun.
He comes to me out on the porch, my shawl he brings
    to warm.
He says that I'm his fancy gal, his strength throughout
    the storm.

I look into his sunburned face, his blue eyes filled
    with light.
I feel the baby move inside, my dress is gettin' tight.
I look into his weathered face and clasp his callused
    hand.
My life looks pretty good tonight, I feel my weddin'
    band.

He leads me back into the house, takes combs from
    my hair.
Sits by the fire, takes me in his lap in the rockin'
    chair.
The children snicker from the loft, spyin' on us from
    above,
I snuggle close inside his arms, his fancy gal, his love.

3 Nov '68

Dear Ashley,

We leave tomorrow morning. Our replacement squadron arrived today, so tonight is a big-time party at the club—everybody in party flight suits, a live band (maybe I'll do a few numbers), and plenty of Mateus wine for all. But the business at hand is to get out of town, so we all are looking for a good night's sleep. There's no reflection today—too much to do. Tomorrow is the day. The airplanes seem to be in good enough shape for the twenty hours of flying ahead. I'm sure we will have a few problems but hope nothing big comes up to delay us. Twenty-four of us air crewmen are anxious to go to the world. As of tomorrow, the chance of getting blowed away decreases dramatically ... so maybe I can get involved here. It sounds to me like you're scared it's real, and you're not ready for the real thing. I've avoided responding to you because of the blowed away factor, but it's hard to ignore responding anymore. Writing to you has been my soft time. All the other time here has been hard time—the heat, the noise, the tension. But I've tried to think through this, and the question that comes is, "Are people meant for each other?" I don't know. We've talked about coincidence and how things happen and what it means, but I've never known anyone like I know you. It's always been a physical attraction with the other girls, but I never really knew what they were all about. I've never seen you, but I understand why you think the way you do. But I'm tired. I'm exhausted from all this getting shot at and working nights. I'm not sure I could hold up my end of an emotional relationship. I need some time to slow down.

So let's make a deal. I won't push you for sex if you don't push me for love. I think we should just enjoy the same company we've enjoyed for a year. I will, however, drink a beer.

Now I'm off to the "O" Club in my blue linen, perfectly tailored, party, flying suit with my combat patches all over the sleeves and chest, to say good-bye.

Love,
Jay

8 Nov '68

Dear Ashley,

We flew twelve airplanes away from Da Nang on the fourth. It was a beautiful sight to see the harbor there in my rearview mirror. That night and the following night, Da Nang was hit by rockets and sappers, so we got out just in time. Right now we are just sitting here at Cubi Point (Subic Bay) in the Philippines waiting for somebody, somewhere, to say we can go home. The proposed schedule calls for us to leave here on Saturday, and we've got twelve airplanes all ready to go. The delay seems to be in scheduling the air refueling tankers for the two legs of the trip that require the tankers.

I had to test a bird yesterday, so I did some sightseeing around this area—Bataan, Leyete, Corrigidor, Manila, Luzon, and many of the other places made famous by wars are all close by, and it was interesting to see the places that had always been just names until now. The islands are beautiful from the air, at about two hundred feet. When I'm on the island, I'm putting the finishing touches on my tan, and my skin resembles that of a full-blooded Indian. Don't be surprised when you see me.

I wish I could hear from you out here in the ocean, especially since I sent that last epistle from Da Nang. There's no telling how you'll react to it, but since I sent it off, it's caused me to think some about things like God. He's sorta gotten lost in the shuffle here. I really do want to buy a little farm and get out of the Marine Corps and go there and stay, and you've pointed out how that might not be realistic. What did the Old Testament dudes do after they busted down all those walls and drank all that wine and stole all that wheat? Did they go back home, hook back up with the old crowd, hang out at the pool room? I've got no plan. Right now it's kinda nice to sit in the sun by the pool on top of the hill overlooking Subic Bay.

Love,
Jay

12 Nov '68

Dear Ashley,

We left Cubi Point yesterday and flew twelve airplanes through bad weather across fifteen hundred miles of ocean to Guam—very tiring. I had vertigo for two hours. I was flying the number-two position on the left wing of the leader in a formation of four airplanes, and for two hours I felt like I was in a screaming dive or a high-angle turn or going straight up, all the while tucked snugly behind my leader's wing. It's quite a sensation to be that confused for that long, not knowing which way is up and having to hold that airplane tight against the other plane while your impulses tell you to break away to avoid crashing.

We were to leave here today for Wake Island, but an unusual late-season storm has forced us to stay here with seventy-five-knot winds and may delay things for a few days. It's a small island, and there's nothing to do, but it is better than Da Nang. The food is great. We're settling into a routine of pinball, whiskey, food, and sleep. We will sit out the storm, check out the airplanes (I'll probably have to test a couple of the birds), go for one night, then gain a day at the date line near Midway (we might air-refuel over Midway instead of landing there), then on to Hawaii where we stop to see how the airplanes are feeling. Then an air-refueling leg to California. This whole operation is interesting, but it lasts too long. It has been a relief for everybody to get away from Vietnam. We were lucky not to lose anybody during the last month there, especially considering how much we got shot at. So everybody in the squadron is relaxing now that the pressure is off. I had thought there would be wild celebration all the way across the ocean, but now that I know I don't have to fly combat anymore, it's just pinball, whiskey, food, and sleep. I'm real tired.

Love,
Jay

18 Nov '68

Dear Ashley,

The aerial view of Wake tells it all—a small place. We finally got away from Guam after five days of wind and rain. Schedule from here on is indefinite now. The airplanes are miraculously hanging together. We will all stay on the beach tonight, with cases of beer, to honor the marines who died here in '42.

Love,
Jay

22 Nov '68

Dear Ashley,

The Pacific Ocean is big. There's no jet stream to help us out, so we're cruising at thirty-six thousand feet but only tracking a ground speed of about 450 knots. Been doing this for days. You drive for four hours in one direction, and the only change is the cloud formations. Below the clouds is the endless blue sea. You talk to your navigator, you talk to the skipper, somebody makes a joke, you have a ham sandwich, and you drive for hours. Then you land and go to flight operations and look at the map, and you're farther away from everything, and the dots in the ocean are getting smaller. Those hours of high-altitude flying are like watching a fire in a fireplace. You tend to become mesmerized, and you stare. It is big, and it is beautiful from way up there.

Hawaii is cool. Technically it's the US but not really the US. The first thing I did was get a burger at McDonalds. This is our third day here, and I haven't slept yet. Some old A-6 drivers at the base have cars, and we've been spending the days on the north-shore beaches and the nights back over the hill in Waikiki. There's just too much to do to think about sleeping, but I'm starting to wind down some. They were having trouble lining up the tankers for the refueling between here and California, so the skipper told us to take a few days, have a nice time. He told us to check in Saturday morning, but some of the people are confused because we gained a day at the date line, and some people are pretty drunk, and some people we've just lost track of. It will probably be Sunday morning before we find everybody and get in good enough shape to fly out of here. Meanwhile, the food is excellent. The weather is perfect, and last night I practiced walking with you on the beach. It was nice, and I had a good time. I'm actually getting kinda excited about seeing you. It will be like getting reacquainted with an old friend. I'll call from California.

Love,
Jay

November 22, 1968

Dear PERI (Probably Eventually Reliable Individual),
    Your "I won't get physical if you don't say you love me" letter surprised me. At that very moment, I decided to take advantage of an opportunity I had been choosing not to let myself consider. (I had heard the "no glove, no love" slogan from a few girls on the hall, but I had never heard your mantra "no love, no need for a glove.") I applied for spring semester abroad in Paris, and your letter and my application just beat the deadline. I've already paid a $250 deposit, so, just like my application to Sylvan Lewis, now I'm committed to a very different college experience next spring. I took French in high school, so this will be a chance to either become fluent or starve to death on the Left Bank because I can't ask for food. Early this fall, I applied for my passport in case I decided Paris was right for me. (You know how I have always wanted to travel.) My work last summer helps me fund the trip, so Mother won't have to pay much more than a semester's tuition. We are spending Christmas in South Carolina at my sister's. I hope I'll get to see you at least once before I go. Classes end here on December 15. Reading day is December 16, my twentieth birthday, and exams end on the twenty-first. I may get out a little early if my exam schedule is a good one. We will go down to my sister's on the twenty-third. Back on the twenty-fifth.
    I leave for Paris on the twenty-ninth, so I'll be spending New Year's in France. Fly over to Paris, and I'll show you Le Tour Eiffel all lit up for the new year. I'm going to stay with a Spanish Countess. Her name is Countess de la Tour d'Amore. Her son is a diplomat, and she takes in exchange students. Her home is near

La Place de Concorde where Marie Antoinette was beheaded. I'm nervous and excited at the same time. I thought I was on my own in Maine, but this time I can't even speak the language. Mother gets teary each time I mention the "Paris Adventure." Even though she would rather I didn't go, she says, "Do things while you're young. Don't miss an opportunity." I am relieved she has that attitude. Daddy would have seen this trip as wasteful and unnecessary.

Here's to honesty, Mr. Pilot. I guess I just don't trust myself with you. I wouldn't want to get a poor little marine pilot in trouble. Plus, you need some time to rediscover yourself, unencumbered, no restrictions, no attachments. (I'm sorry if I seemed too pushy. I was feeling lonely and wishing you were here when I wrote the last letter.) I still wish you were here, but your readjustment to the world will be better without me to complicate your thought processes. If you want to get away from Cherry Point for a weekend, I am sure Jena and Annie will be glad to show you around school. Some of my guy friends will let you stay with them. I will return early in May. Of course I will be returning as a woman of the world. I thought maybe I could get a job dancing at the Moulin Rouge. Do you think those French folks would be interested in learning the Carolina shag?

Your letters have brought me great joy this past year. You have helped me become more independent and sure of myself. I am planning and then doing, like you said.

"No love, no need for a glove,"
Ashley

January 24, 1969

Dearest Jay,

I have waited to write to you so my thoughts could be clearer. It seems like a lifetime since that cold and snowy December day you called. Your timing was good. We sat across from each other at the café in Raleigh, playing with our food, studying how we each talked, held our forks, dropped our eyes, coughed through a silence. I know you made a special effort to grab those few hours we spent together at some risk to your career, given the circumstances of your short leave time. As I think about the day, it all felt awkward. I was cold, sneezing every few minutes, and you were worried about the time it would take to get back to base that afternoon. I know I wasn't the best company and a big disappointment to a war hero like you. I wish we could have had a few days to interact and get to know each other as we had hoped. You said, "There is a reason for everything in the master plan we call our lives." Perhaps you are right. Perhaps those days we had planned to spend together were not part of the master plan. I was not disappointed in the person sitting across from me, and if I close my eyes, I can bring back the feel and warmth of your hand on mine and the strength in your embrace. I even liked the way our lips softened together for that one brief kiss. I saw the intensity in your eyes as you talked about the farm you planned to buy. I can't remember the food I ate or didn't eat. I remember feeling hungry when you drove away, though, and I can see in my mind's eye the huge snowflakes cooling my tearful cheeks. I don't remember getting in the car, and I'll never know how I got out of the parking lot or managed to drive home through the blinding snow. It all seems so surreal as I think back. It's been more than a month, and I still can't fathom how a year's worth of writing and dreaming and thinking of you came to two hours in a dinky diner with a Blue Plate Special. I hope you find what you are looking for and are happy with your choices. My year with you by mail was total joy.

My flight to Paris was uneventful and long. I snoozed a little but was too excited to rest much. I caught a train from Orly Airport to Gare du Nord, and from there the metro to Place de la Concorde. My fifth-floor room is several streets west of the metro stop. As I told you before, I am staying with the Countess de la Tour d'Amore. She is Spanish. She lives on the first floor that is really the second floor by our standards. Her apartment is filled with French Provincial furniture. She has a short, stocky son who works as a diplomat with the Spanish Embassy. She draped herself across a fainting couch when she talked to me before sending me up four flights of steps to the servants' quarters. The room is cold and has a sink with cold water. The WC (water closet) is down the steps midway between the fourth and fifth floors. It has no shower. I am sharing a room with another exchange student from the United States. Her name is Angeline, and she lives somewhere near New Orleans. Thus far I have seen no voodoo dolls. She is very homesick, and I'm not sure she will survive the semester.

This time I am not homesick. I have so much to see, and the classes have been delightful. I am quickly learning to understand French, although I cannot speak it very well. I usually eat lunch at a small restaurant down the street and buy fruit and snacks for the evening. I take the metro to three afternoon classes at the Sorbonne. I have one morning class that meets two days a week. I am studying the language, the history, the arts, and the literature of France in class, and I am studying the people everywhere I go. I have been to the Louvre twice and to the Impressionist Gallery in the Garden of the Tuileries once.

There is so much to see. Last night I was on my way home when I wound up walking behind a black woman with tiny braided hair extensions that practically touched the ground. She had beads in the braids and walked on stiletto heels. I imagined she was a dancer at the Moulin Rouge or the Follies, but I will probably never know. She was stunning, and everyone on the street turned to watch her, men and women alike.

Paris is such an amazing city! It truly is the City of Lights. I don't think anyone ever goes to bed except me, and sometimes I, too, stay up very late to drink in this city.

The French readings are slow for me, as you can imagine. I sometimes go out for coffee in the early morning and study in the warmth of a corner booth in a pastry shop a few streets away. The manager is a kind man, over fifty, mustached, and his face is creased from the constant smile he wears. He occasionally gives me a sweet roll that is leftover from yesterday, and I devour it. His wife helps me with words I don't understand because she has studied English. She is plump, always wears a fresh white apron, and her cheeks have powdery smudges of flour no matter what time of day I see her. I'm always finding flour smudges in my text after she has helped me. They have a daughter who is studying in Germany. I think I remind them of her, or they hope their kindness to me will engender kindness to her in Berlin. If she is anything like they are, she will draw kindness from everyone she meets. They have offered their daughter's room if I need it. I like being in the pastry shop when I choose and not having to explain my comings and goings as I might feel obligated to do if I lived with them.

I am broadening my circle of friends with each class. People in the classes are from everywhere, so I am experiencing many cultural differences. So far I haven't been brave enough to go out on a date. There have been many group outings to various museums followed by long, lingering meals at moderately priced restaurants. Talking with the group has improved my French.

My hands are cold. I have on gloves and a coat, but I still feel the cold through my coat. There will be no sunbathing in a bikini for me in Paris this winter. My stark little room has one small, dirty window. I sit in the small window seat and watch the comings and goings below. The family across the way has three small children who go to the park with a nanny every morning at ten. Two men live together in another apartment. I think they are lovers. In another apartment, a young woman lives with an older man. During the day, a young man visits while the older gentleman is at work. I often witness fights, and occasionally a plate or pan flies through the window of another apartment. A vegetable vendor pushes a cart through the street early each morning. He is usually my first alarm clock. French men leer at me on the metro. One day I stood at the pole near the door of the train, and a tall, young workman put his hand over mine on the pole. Every time I moved my hand, he moved his, licked his lips, and smirked, bringing guffaws of laughter from his friend. I tried to avoid his eyes. Luckily his stop was ahead of mine.

I hope you are well and are adjusting nicely to the North Carolina winter. I wish you could fly over here, but I know that is just wishful thinking. If there is a master plan, I am supposed to be here at this time. I thought my trip to Maine was unbelievable, but this experience in Paris is life changing. I am thinking about majoring in International Studies next year. I assume I could work in an embassy in some glamorous corner of the world for a while after college. I hope to go to Italy and travel a bit with a few of the students in my classes in late March. Many of my classmates have traveled a good bit, and they seem very happy to show me the world. I tried to smoke a cigarette with a holder the other night at a bar near the campus. Each of us was trying to outvamp the other, talking with exaggerated accents, leaning on the piano. The locals laughed with us and at us. There seemed to be less hostility toward Americans that night than I have seen. Maybe because most of the patrons at the bar were college age. It's the midtwenties to midthirties crowd that appears to despise us. I knew they hated the English, but I didn't realize how much they hated us too.

Thank you again for making the effort to see me before my trip. You are in my heart, and I wish you the best. It is funny how far away I feel. I'm actually closer than I was last year, but it feels far.

Love,
Ashley

The Eiffel Tower, Paris.

The Moulin Rouge, Paris.

February 24, 1969

Dear Ashley,

Dinky diner with a Blue Plate Special? Been going there since I was twelve! My friend Chuck and I started a grass-cutting business when we were ten, got us some neighbors' grass to cut, and we saved our money for two years. The first thing we did when we had some money was buy tickets on the big dog. Greyhound ran from Piedmont to Raleigh and back on Saturdays for a buck eighty. So we took the bus to Raleigh one Saturday and ate lunch—the same meatloaf I had with you—then we took in a movie and rode the afternoon dog back to Piedmont. It was our idea of a good time.

Once I saw you, I knew we're supposed to be friends for life. Your letters were important to me at Da Nang. Now it looks like your experience abroad will be different from what I ran into. I'd like to know how it turns out. I'm transitioning to the A-4M next week and will get carrier qualified on the USS Lexington out of Pensacola. Then I'll be an LSO—Landing Signal Officer—the man who stands on the ass-end of an aircraft carrier and tells the pilots how to land. I'll be floating around the North Atlantic for the next few years, freezing in the winter, toasting in the summer, trying to keep all those airplane drivers alive. When I'm out there in the ocean, controlling airplanes, I'll wave to you international-jet-setter-intellectuals as you travel by. You can see the carrier in the ocean—a postage stamp with a white streak behind it cutting through the waves and flights of fighters swarming overhead.

You are a beautiful lady.

Fondly,
Jay

March 10, 1969

Dear Blue Plate Special Speck in the Ocean,

My mother makes the best meatloaf I've ever eaten. She puts tomato soup on top and even grates carrots inside with all the other fantastic ingredients that make it scrumptious. I love it, and I'll never be such a "super intellectual" that I fail to enjoy her meatloaf. By the way, I also like brie. Is the problem the diner or the distance between us?

I have moved to an apartment that a friend of mine is staying in while the owners are out of town. It has high ceilings and lovely old chandeliers that shimmer when the light hits the crystal. I actually have my own bedroom and heat and a bath with a footed tub and shower. The comforter on my bed has a silk duvet covering it, and the bed is big and soft and wraps itself around me when I crawl in at night. The kitchen has huge floor-to-ceiling windows that overlook a central courtyard. It's only two blocks from the school. My body is beginning to thaw, and I feel close to human again. I miss my cold sponge baths and my early morning run to the WC only to be beaten by this strange little man who lived on the fourth floor. It was his greatest joy in life to keep me shivering on the steps while he lingered in the john. I think he could hear my door close as I left my room, and he would deliberately set out to make my day start miserably while he warmed the commode seat. Is paranoia real or something we create to understand the difficulties we face? I am so grateful now for the little comforts I used to take for granted.

I'm sorry I can't be in North Carolina to get to know you. My demons are strong, and I have to figure out who I am before I make any decisions that commit me for life—even lifelong friendship. While we were in the restaurant, you talked about the fear you felt during your sojourn in Vietnam. My fear is that I will never find myself, that I will never know what I was sent to this earth to accomplish. Right now I don't have a clue. Sometimes I think I'm a fluke, that my brother wasn't supposed to die, and I wasn't supposed to be. But here I am sitting in the study in this fabulous Paris apartment, writing at an eighteenth-century desk with leather inlay on the top, surrounded by the musty smell of old books, written in French, pouring out my soul to someone who is angry because I called his meatloaf a Blue Plate Special.

By the way, I was thinking of you as I wrote this poem at that very desk.

> Above the clouds, moonlight beams
> Hiding shadows, hiding rain below;
> Tears from heaven.
> If I can stay above the fray,
> Disconnected, free of pain.
> If I can live another day.
> If I can find you in the peace.
> If I can find solace in one deceitful moment,
> I can return to the tears, to the rain.
> I am not lost; I am found.

> by ABJ

I hope I see you again when we both understand a little more about this life we're living. I wish you all good things: farms, dogs, meatloaf, and as many airplanes as you can fly. Did you know if you had turned around and come back to me on that cold, snowy December day, I would have gone with you forever?

Ashley

Epilogue

After midnight, December 1, 2001

Jay read her last line again, over and over as he had so many years before. He then picked up the worn postcard he had never sent—worn because he had carried it in his back pocket for months before putting it with her letters. He looked at the words he had written. "If you had just called my name, I would have stayed with you. I love you, Ashley."

Jay Fox took off his glasses, touched his moist eyes and face with *her* red bandanna, carefully rewrapped the letters, placed them in the file cabinet, picked up his lantern, and headed to the house.

Acknowledgments

First, I wish to thank my husband, Tim, for his support in proofreading and getting the manuscript in the proper form for publication. He spent countless hours on this task and never ceased to laugh appropriately at parts of the novel, no matter how many times he read it. I am also thankful to Laurel Goldman, acclaimed novelist and teacher, who critiqued the novel early in the process and gave excellent advice. To my friend Merrie Hedrick, thank you for your continued encouragement. In addition, I appreciate the support of my book club friends, Dava Abbott, Maggie Andersen, Lois Campbell, Lynn Davis, Sally Gadd, Karen Hansen, Beth Jones, Patti McAnally, Loye Messina, Janet Monteith, Pam Moore, Susan Toler Rogers, Nancy Thompson, and Nell Yates, who introduced me to amazing authors, which made me a better writer. They patiently encouraged me to take the step of publishing (even if they didn't know they did).

Two Vietnam veterans provided substantial support, and I am extremely grateful for their contributions to this book. Don Martin shared many of his personal photos with me. These wonderful pictures of his year "in country" related directly to so much of what Jay Fox, the young pilot, talked about in the novel. The story comes alive when looking at Don's pictures. Lieutenant Colonel Jim Dyer, US Army (Retired), read the novel, wanted to see it published, and encouraged me because, as a Vietnam veteran, he so related to the story.

I wish I could thank my late mother, Marjorie Bowles Watson, who read *Gulliver's Travels* to me when I was five. She opened my eyes to great literature and was always a source of strength and encouragement. Finally, I want to thank G. C. "Pete" Hendricks, a great writer, who agreed to partner with me in writing this epistolary novel. It was an exciting and meaningful experience to work with Pete in bringing these two characters to life as they explored their lives in relation to the war and each other.

About the Authors

To Any Soldier was written by G. C. "Pete" Hendricks, author of the critically acclaimed novel *The Second War* (Viking, 1990), and Kathryn Watson Quigg, a published poet, artist, and guest commentator on NPR. This epistolary novel, while not autobiographical, is grounded in their personal experiences.

Mr. Hendricks is a decorated marine attack pilot with more than two hundred missions in Vietnam. He has taught creative writing at both Duke University and North Carolina State University and was selected as the Tar Heel of the Week by the Raleigh *News and Observer* for his environmental contributions in the field of deconstruction. He is the father of Holly and grandfather of Olivia. He currently lives in Bigfork, Montana.

Ms. Quigg is a past chair of the Wake County Board of Education, the nation's sixteenth-largest school system, and has

received several awards including the Stanley Frank Leadership Award from North Carolina Leadership 2000 and the Friend of Education Award in 2005 from Wake County NCAE. She has a BA in English from Wake Forest University and a M.Ed. from the University of North Carolina at Chapel Hill. Kathryn is a watercolor artist and certified reality therapist, and she has a first-degree black belt in Tae Kwon Do. She lives in Wake Forest, North Carolina, with her husband, Tim. They have one adult son, Seth.

CPSIA information can be obtained
at www.ICGtesting.com
Printed in the USA
LVOW11s0255251016
510131LV00001B/74/P

"I could not put the book down and read it cover
veteran, spouse, or friend of a veteran, for or against our involvement in Vietnam,
knows the importance of Mail Call."

—**Lt. Col. Jim Dyer,** US Army, retired

In 1968 Jay Fox is a young marine attack pilot in Vietnam and Ashley Beth Justice is a college freshman in North Carolina when they meet each other by chance, through letters.

Ashley Beth, naïve and totally separated from the Vietnam War, begins her letter-writing as a way to personally contribute to the war effort. Having recently moved away from her small hometown, she's beginning to see the world from a new perspective.

Jay, in the midst of bombing runs each evening, has purposefully distanced himself from any close relationships, but there's something about Ashley Beth's innocent and forthright manner that compels him to answer her letters.

The reality of the war hits home for Ashley Beth when Jay describes his plane almost colliding with another after a dangerous bombing run. The stakes are higher now—the disagreements, more intense; the flirtations, more significant.

Even amid the bloodshed in Vietnam and the civil unrest at home, Jay and Ashley Beth dare to dream of a life together while struggling to understand the war and themselves in *To Any Soldier.*

G. C. HENDRICKS, the critically acclaimed author of *The Second War,* is a decorated pilot who flew more than two hundred missions in Vietnam. He lives and works in Montana.

KATHRYN WATSON QUIGG, an artist and writer who lives in North Carolina, has worked in mental health, and education, and was an elected member and chair of the Wake County Board of Education.

U.S. $17.95

ISBN 978-1-4917-6873-0

9 781491 768730